TRUE Love

Dr. Sudhakar Ancha

NEWMAN SPRINGS PUBLISHING
320 Broad Street
Red Bank, NJ 07701

First originally published by Newman Springs Publishing 2023

ISBN 979-8-88763-741-9 (Paperback)
ISBN 979-8-88763-742-6 (Digital)

Printed in the United States of America

To my family and friends who inspired and
encouraged me to write this novel

Chapter

1

The alarm went off.

Kristen managed to pick up her heavy head and reach for the resonating alarm clock.

In the close distance of the other room, her roommate, Cathy, was once again annoyed by the familiar noise she repeatedly hears every morning. It's frustrating to Cathy. It brought childhood memories, as it is the same sound that rings from her own mother's room when she was young.

Kristen always chuckled at this response from Cathy. The two would even try to play some sick game as to who will win being the resilient, a yet satisfying showdown between the two. They were inseparable though. Knowing each other through college, they became best friends, maybe even better, distant sisters. They attended college in Dansville, Illinois, where Kristen prepared herself for the road ahead.

Kristen now worked for a health insurance company, where her degree and skills are put to the test. Cathy reluctantly got a job, thanks to Kristen's charisma as she wooed her bosses. Cathy always appreciated Kristen because she would lay down her life for a friend.

Every day, Kristen would take the subway train out of Loyola College station to her office downtown. She took this time to reflect on her day and her life on those tracks.

Cathy was batching up a brew for Kristen. She always knew that's what got her day started. If it weren't for the coffee, there would be no forward progress. The two girls had been roommates for two years now. Not that they didn't have their ups and downs, because everyone does, but they developed a relationship that no circumstances or any man could separate. They chose to love and be loved.

"I'm heading out," Kristen spoke.

"I'm right behind you," Cathy responded.

"It's getting late, you better hurry," Kristen replied.

"Yes, I will. Love you," Cathy responded.

Kristen threw her briefcase over her shoulder and exited with a smooch from her lips in the distance. Cathy responded the same.

* * * * *

The train station downtown at the Loyola College station was always packed to the brim with onlookers, including different types of people coming from wide-ranging backgrounds. One thing was common though, the hustle and bustle of getting to work on time. Kristen, coming from a little town in Potomac, Illinois, whose population was less than a thousand, possessed an easy-living patience that no city folk could accomplish. She chuckled to see the people resembling packrats that are looking for a way inside once the doors to the subway train opened. She just filed in line behind the funnel of people that were all looking to make their entrance.

Every morning, she was lucky to get a seat. Most of the time she would stand with her fingers holding the hooks in the ceiling dangling in the air. Sometimes, her backside would rest right up against an onlooker in the seat next to her. She even caught herself silently laughing as both herself and the person next to her felt a little uncomfortable. She always found an opportunity to make the best of everything. It was just in the DNA of Kristen.

The beauty of Kristen was always appreciated by people around her. She was an attractive woman in her midtwenties, with blond hair and blue eyes, something you would see in a model. Her facial features were very sharp. Her smile was contagious. Her character reflected her beauty. Anyone would want to get to know her.

Kristen was a lot like her mother. They were very close growing up. Kristen's mother made her to go to Sunday school without fail.

Her mom could have been very strict. She was always the center of attention. Kristen, on the other hand, was the center of attraction. And being the first girl on her mom's side, she led the pack with her stature. Kristen missed her mom though. Once Kristen moved to the city and reached for her dreams, her mom was left back in Potomac and yielded to her normal living back home. Kristen thought about her a lot.

Kristen's cell phone rang. It was Michael.

"Hello, my dear," Kristen spoke.

"What are you up to, hon?" Michael asked.

"Getting off the subway, heading to work," Kristen replied.

Hearing Michael's voice always brought her back to the time they met. It was three years ago when they first locked eyes. They met at a colleague's birthday party. Though Kristen didn't seem interested whatsoever, Michael was diligent to get to know her on an intimate level, and he was able to capture her digits that evening. Michael invited her to dinner the following week. Even though Kristen was checked out and gave every excuse as to why she could not go to dinner, eventually, Michael scored and Kristen buckled to his request.

They met at one of the fanciest steakhouses in the city. Michael was a show-off by nature, and maybe that's why Kristen gave in to the temptation. Michael was a computer programmer for a software company. He made a good salary, which gave him a lot of wiggle room to impress Kristen.

During dinner, the two hit it off. They were like Chatty Cathy, passing the time talking about their livelihoods that neither of them knew they had so much passion for in the first place. Michael appeared nervous at first, which was outside of his nature. Kristen began to like Michael. She thought of him as being genuine and to the point. Kristen's lifestyle seemed to match a lot of Michael's life. Inasmuch as Kristen cared for others, she could tell Michael felt the same way, even by the way he tipped his waitress as they finished their night.

Michael was in his late twenties, five foot and eight inches tall with a physical build. He had an undaunting smile and was beyond charming. Michael's work ethic matched his personality as he was very hardworking and always gave the best for his company. That's the thing, he seemed like a well-put-together gentleman, and Kristen had struck gold to know him.

"Okay, honey, I will call you later," Michael assured as they said goodbye.

"Love you," Kristen spoke.

Kristen had finally reached her work. In her always-on-time entrance, everyone greeted Kristen with a smile and nod. She displayed the typical, universal good-to-see-you body language at her job. Kristen was always adored by all those around her. She carried a charisma that others thought to be authentic and genuine. It was probably the reason Kristen's boss hired her years ago.

Kristen had to get ready for her morning meeting, where she was to lead the presentation. She was always a nervous Nellie at first. But when she gained her composure, Kristen was flawless.

Her phone went off. It was Michael.

"Are you free for lunch?" Michael asked.

"Sorry, honey, I have more meetings aligned throughout the day," Kristen replied.

"That's okay. I'll see you tonight?" Michael asked.

"Yes, that would be fine. Love you," Kristen replied.

* * * * *

Because of Kristen's busy schedule, she only found time to eat at the cafeteria for lunch. But she didn't mind. Coming from a small town, she didn't mind a sandwich and chips at all.

Crystal, a coworker and friend, announced from across the room, "Hey you!"

"Oh, hey, Crystal," Kristen replied.

"Are you excited about the big day?" Crystal asked.

"I am, Crystal," Kristen replied.

Michael had proposed to Kristen. They dated for three years before getting engaged about one year ago. The whole company knew. Her family knew. Even Tom, a coworker who had a crush on Kristen, knew.

The problem is that Kristen was overwhelmed by the number of things that needed to be done leading up to the wedding: the venue where the service is to be held, the photographer, the dress, and every detail in between. Nevertheless, Kristen was determined to make her day big for both Michael and her.

Kristen grew up in a very traditional Catholic church. She held on to her values. She didn't believe in sex before marriage and announced this to Michael at the beginning of their relationship. She was an only child, so it left a lot of room for her parents to instill core values into her life.

However, she never knew her father. She had some very minimal memories of a man living in their house as a child, but she didn't recall a father being at her side. Her mom always explained that her dad was never in her life because of the choices he made when she was still young. Kristen thought about her father.

Kristen called Michael.

"Hey, I'm heading home," Kristen spoke.

"Okay, finishing up here at work and I will meet you there," Michael responded.

"Sounds good honey. Love you," Kristen spoke.

"Love you too," Michael responded.

Kristen had to hightail it to the subway to catch the train. This was always her time to reflect on her day and the blessings of having the people that she had in her life. The subway always conjured up a diverse crowd—the spotless businessman in his three-piece suit; the underdressed alternative crowd who hardly engaged with others; the young, overworked mother who worked three jobs just to keep her children fed; the poor folks who were always panhandling on the sidewalks just to get through another day.

Kristen had an underlying compassion for the homeless. She always thought of them as being down on their luck and felt sorry for the situation they are facing in their lives. Somewhere deep in her heart she wondered how they became homeless. While getting off the train, she always made it a point to give them a couple of dollars.

Loyola Station was always Kristen's oasis. She used the subway as her counseling session to reflect, to decompress, and to think about her future. She wondered at times if she was going to be all right. But somewhere down deep in her heart, she knew she would be.

Kristen had just exited the train when she suddenly felt a shift in her arm. Looking down, she noticed her purse was gone from her hands.

"Hey!" Kristen yelled in the distance. "That's my purse!"

The two young teenagers had bolted into the distance, racing off with Kristen's purse in hand, confident they had gotten away. But an African American man stopped them in their tracks and tackled one guy while the other one had flipped over the two. They were grappling and fighting for the prize.

Seeing them scrambling with one another, Kristen was frantic as to whether she should do something or not. She was yelling for help, but at this point, they were too far from the subway for anyone to hear. She was pacing around the fight. Like a pack of ravaging wolves, their arms and legs looked like a sick twister game that no one had a chance at victory.

Out of nowhere, the African American man stood up with the purse in his hands, and the two young men ran off in the distance, disappearing into the woods.

"Thank you so much," Kristen said, relieved.

"You're welcome," the man replied.

"What's your name?" Kristen asked.

"It's James." He's a retired boxing coach, who appears to be in his sixties. He said, "I actually live in the same complex where you live."

"Really?" Kristen replied. "I can't thank you enough."

"You just stay safe out there," James replied.

Chicago was not a walk-in-the-park city. It came with opportunity, but it also came with great darkness as well. The addicted, the poor, the prideful—they all resided in this place. Kristen was seeing this darkness within the city for the first time. It almost brought a little anxiety to her, coming from such a safe town growing up.

Kristen safely walked into her apartment and slumped on the sofa.

"Are you okay?" Cathy asked.

"Yeah, just exhausted," Kristen replied.

"What happened today?" Cathy asked.

"Well, let's just say I almost had my purse stolen," Kristen replied.

"You're kidding me?" Cathy responded.

"Nope. But we're all good now," Kristen replied.

Cathy always looked out for Kristen, and Kristen was like a mother to Cathy. The two were inseparable.

"Are you excited for the wedding?" Cathy asked.

"Oh yes, I can't wait!" Kristen replied.

The wedding was eight weeks away. Ready or not, Kristen knew this was going to be her special day. Even when she was younger, she imagined herself dressed to the gills in white, walking down the aisle, and holding her bouquet. She just knew in her heart Michael was the one.

Chapter

2

Michael was swift to pick up Kristen in his usual over-the-top arrival.

Dining became a commodity to the two. They used food as a prime pivotal point in their relationship. Michael loved dishing it out, and Kristen succumbed to the offers.

"You look very nice, my dear," Michael spoke eloquently.

"Not too bad yourself, mister," Kristen replied.

"You two have fun!" Cathy shouted in the distance.

Michael was escorting Kristen to the usual steakhouse located on Main Street. It was above-par dining, which accentuated Michael's personality. The two always found time to talk about their endless days and the conversations that they had with others. Kristen loved Michael, and Michael adored Kristen. They were closely becoming the perfect match.

The wedding became the prime topic.

"Are you getting excited about the wedding?" Michael asked.

"Yes, of course, Michael," Kristen answered.

"I'm thinking we should go to Cancun for our honeymoon," Michael said.

"That sounds wonderful," Kristen replied.

"I found an awesome secluded place for us to have all to ourselves." Michael winked.

Kristen could feel the excitement bubbling up within. All her dreams, her desires, her focus were circling around this big day. She gazed into the eyes of Michael as if he was like a chatty schoolboy asking his high school sweetheart to prom. Except for the letterman jacket, Michael had a sense of youth still in him.

"My wedding gown will be ready in three weeks," Kristen announced.

"That's exciting!" Michael spoke. "So you said yes to the dress?"

"Yes! I go back in a couple weeks to make sure it's tailored right," Kristen replied.

Even though her big day was coming into order, Kristen had a lot of nervousness around it all. Will her dress "wow" Michael? Will she be the perfect wife for him? Much of Kristen's life was wrapped around disappointment. This is something she carried with her throughout her life. She never knew her father, which made her feel that she'd never be adequate for any man. This is something silly she pondered from time to time as a young girl growing up.

"Don't worry, honey," Michael spoke. "Everything will be all right."

It's like Michael was reading Kristen's thoughts. Michael gently slid his hand across the table to grab Kristen's hand. There was always comfort in Michael's touch. Kristen always melted at the still touch of Michael's skin.

The waitress came back to their table.

"Will that be all?" the waitress spoke.

"Yes, we are ready for our ticket," Michael replied gently.

Michael always took the lead. It was in his nature from birth. Not that he was some overbearing narcissist with no compassion for others, but he just liked to be the dominate one. This is something that was attractive to Kristen.

"Hey, let's get out of here and go get some ice cream," Michael suggested.

"That sounds wonderful," Kristen replied.

"There's a Baskin Robbins across the street." Michael pointed.

They left the steakhouse and headed toward the exit in their fashionably romantic way, with Kristen's head perched on Michael's shoulder and Michael's dominant hand over Kristen's. The two of them were truly in love.

After their after-hour ice cream and continually talking about the wedding, Michael and Kristen were spent. Michael dropped Kristen off at her apartment. And after his courteous open-the-door practice, Michael walked Kristen to her front door, and the two ended their night with a kiss.

* * * * *

Friday night happened.

Kristen was awakened in a panic, disturbed by the dream she just had. Cathy ran into her bedroom, awakened by the commotion that was happening.

"Are you all right, Kristen?" Cathy shouted.

"I must've had a bad dream," Kristen replied.

Kristen's heart was pounding. She felt a shortness of breath from her night terror. Cathy attempted to calm Kristen down.

"You need to relax," Cathy spoke.

Kristen had dealt with her night terrors before. Uncertain how and why she had them, Kristen felt helpless at times, imprisoned by the visions that she'd get. Half the time she couldn't remember them but still be awakened anyway, knowing that they did happen.

"Here, drink some water," Cathy said.

"You are so sweet, Cathy," Kristen replied.

Cathy was Kristen's saving grace. Every time Kristen had panic attacks, Cathy was always available to help her get through them. Kristen loved Cathy as her roommate, but more, as her best friend. Cathy always knew how to calm Kristen down.

* * * * *

The next morning Cathy made her usual gourmet breakfast and left a small note for Kristen. The notes always consisted of daily reminders as to why Cathy appreciated Kristen so much.

Kristen exited her apartment and headed to the subway station.

As usual, the train arrived on time. The sound of the screeching metal wheels of the train forced Kristen to step forward. The onlookers synchronized with Kristen's steps as they all anticipated the next boarding. Without fail, the admirers smiled at Kristen, and she returned the favor.

Kristen would always find that one empty seat next to a window so she could go back to her oasis. The train shifted forward as Kristen's eyes panned across the onlookers waiting for their next ride. As the train gained forward motion, Kristen gazed upon the old and new buildings parading across the city. The contrast of rich and poor neighborhoods was eye-opening to Kristen.

How could there be so much diversity squeezed into such a small space? she thought.

The sounds of the tracks that played like piano notes, turning to a beautiful song, repeated in Kristen's head. The tall Sears Tower and the other skyscrapers were like juggernauts overlooking the city. Chicago was home to her. Kristen understood that in life, some people have big dreams that play out while others must work hard to make their dreams come true by luck.

Kristen always wondered what it was like to live on the luxurious side of Chicago. The Drake Towers and Michigan Avenue were places the wealthy lived and only the rich survived.

The train came to a stop.

Kristen's thoughts suddenly shifted, and the spell of fantasy was broken. Kristen made her way through the double steel doors and exited the train. Like usual, there are a few homeless people waiting in the corridors of the boarding entrance, stuck between the trenches of life. Kristen made her usual donation of a few dollars for the less fortunate.

"Thank you, ma'am. God bless you," the homeless man spoke.

"Have a nice day," Kristen replied.

Kristen had compassion for the less fortunate. Deep inside her heart she had this hidden agenda to help those in need. Maybe it stemmed from her childhood when Kristen's mother always told her to be kind to people and help those in need. Either way, Kristen would have given the shirt off her back for a stranger.

Looking back at the homeless man, she thought of ways to help him. And if need be, she wanted to help him gravitate his life to a better place. She pondered upon his half-torn jacket. *Had he gotten it from the local thrift shop or grabbed it out of a garbage disposal in a hidden alley?* Seeing the homeless man's ragged hairstyle halfway covering his face and the broken eyes that peeped through his dreads, accumulated from the countless nights of not showering, only made Kristen wish even more that there was a way to save the homeless.

Kristen finally made her way to the office. Interrupted by the different people seeking her attention, Kristen noticed a large bouquet of flowers stationed right on top of her desk. She was surprised and opened the envelope.

It read, "*Thinking of you. Love, Michael.*"

Kristen was bashful, to say the least. She knew Michael was confident, but never did she see this side of his nature.

Kristen had to get ready for her plethora of meetings that she had planned out for the day. But for the life of her, she simply could not keep from thinking about her wedding. Maybe it was the combination of Michael's charm from dinner last night and the surprise beautiful flowers that kept her distracted.

The phone rang. It was Kristen's mother.

"Hey, Mom," Kristen greeted.

"How are you doing?" Kristen's mom asked.

"Well, I'm here at work getting all my meetings planned," Kristen replied.

"I was wondering how the arrangements are coming along for the wedding," her mom asked.

"Things are well. Michael and Cathy are helping me," Kristen replied.

"Okay, I just worry about you, you know?" her mom responded.

"I know. Things will be fine. I must go. Love you," Kristen spoke.

The rest of the day was uneventful. Kristen completed all her meetings, made all the connections she needed for the day, and then headed home. Kristen was exhausted. She hightailed it to Loyola Station to catch the subway.

* * * * *

As the days grew closer to her wedding, Kristen became exceedingly stressed. Michael tried to reassure her, but Kristen always felt like something was missing.

"You look so tense lately," Michael said.

"I feel stressed for some reason," Kristen responded.

"Why is that?" Michael asked.

"It's because I know your father wanted you to marry someone else," Kristen said.

Michael's father wanted him to marry his best friend's daughter. She was the school's most adored student. She was well rounded, athletic, kept a good reputation, and was mesmerizing to the eyes. Kristen felt inadequate about meeting his father's standards. She never had the confidence of becoming the woman Michael's parents envisioned for him. The two, to Michael's dad, never seemed like a perfect match. Then again, Michael didn't seem to be a match made in heaven to Kristen either.

Kristen deeply wanted to appeal to Michael's father, even though he didn't approve of their wedding from the start.

"Well, he will have to get over it," Michael boldly spoke.

The conversation took a turn when Michael's eyes met Kristen's beauty. Her blue eyes were glowing from the nighttime moon. Her blond hair reminded him of a warm, sunshine-filled day while running through the fields of wheat when he was growing up as a kid. The sharp features of Kristen's face captured Michael's attention on a regular basis. None of the conversation mattered anymore. Michael knew Kristen was the one for him, the one he waited for all his life.

Chapter

3

There was just three weeks left until the wedding.

Everything leading up to this point was going to have to work. Kristen was forcing herself to keep her composure. As much as she wanted to scream at times, under the surface she kept it together for Michael.

Michael was a dream for Kristen that became a reality. And Kristen's thoughts about him were good. Never in a million years did Kristen envisioned herself with him, and now she couldn't imagine a life without him. Michael's breathtaking courage kept her stable, and his complete leadership in the workplace played a role in their relationship. In Kristen's thinking, Michael was the perfect package for her and something she couldn't wait to unwrap one day.

"Do you think your parents would be okay with taking care of the reception bill?" Kristen asked.

"I haven't talked to them about it yet," Michael stated. "But I don't see it being a problem."

Michael's parents grew up wealthy. His father worked for Microsoft. Coincidently, Michael's father worked with the same woman he wanted Michael to marry, which to Kristen seemed to make things worse. Michael was always raised to work hard, play hard, and thrive throughout life. These were characteristics that Michael still held tight to very strongly in his adulthood.

"I hope you are not changing your mind at the last minute because of your parents' pressure?" Kristen asked.

"No, silly," Michael responded. "Let's not talk about that. You know you're the one for me."

"Okay," Kristen said.

"Now, how many are we expecting?" Michael asked.

"Around 150," Kristen replied.

Kristen didn't need a glamorous wedding. She was okay with a simple ceremony. Michael could have cared less. He had one thing on his mind—Kristen walking down the aisle dressed eloquently in her white gown.

Chicago was known for its deep-dish pizza, called pies by outsiders. Kristen, growing up in a small town from Chicago, never knew food like this existed. Michael showed Kristen all the secret places to dine in Chicago, and she came to love this popular pie.

"Wow, it's already ten p.m.!" Kristen announced.

"Yeah, let's get you home," Michael replied.

The popular Lakeshore Drive ride home during the night was common ground for Michael and Kristen. Chicago's skyscrapers garnished the city life with its tall, luxurious, and overpowering buildings. Kristen's arm dangled out the window to catch the nighttime air and help her enhance the experience. Kristen loved taking in all the palpable emotions she felt while glaring at Michael's profile and thinking, *Fairy tales do come true.*

Michael dropped Kristen off in his usual gentlemanly role. He opened the door for Kristen and kissed her good night.

"Thank you for another beautiful evening," Kristen said.

"You're welcome, my dear," Michael replied.

Kristen used her key to open the front door and met Cathy in their apartment.

"Where were you?" Cathy asked.

"I was with Michael," Kristen replied. "He took me out for pizza again."

"So are you all set for the wedding?" Cathy asked.

"I'm a little nervous," Kristen responded.

"Why do you say that?" Cathy asked.

"Michael's father doesn't necessarily approve of the wedding," Kristen responded.

"Well, I can understand your fears," Cathy said.

"I trust Michael," Kristen said.

"By the way, don't forget that we are going to Kim's house tomorrow for a birthday," Cathy announced.

"Oh yes, I remember now," Kristen responded. "Any special occasion?"

"It's Stephanie's thirtieth birthday," Cathy replied.

Cathy explained to Kristen that Stephanie had been through a lot recently. A few months ago, her divorce was finalized. Stephanie had caught her husband in an affair with her best friend, which, for anyone, would be traumatizing.

For some reason, this only increased Kristen's anxiety. She thought, *What if that were to happen to me? I don't know if I could live without Michael, even under the most absurd situation.* "I feel sorry for her," Kristen said.

"She's getting better every day," Cathy replied.

"Time does heal," Kristen said.

Cathy had gone to bed as Kristen sat there in her pajamas, watching late-night television. Kristen was beside herself. Her mind filled with questions and doubts. She thought of how shifting life can be.

Take Stephanie's story as an example. A woman, fully in love, finds her husband having an affair with her best friend. But now she's on the roadway to recovery. She has her house, the cars, but, luckily, no children. Even so, the situation kept Kristen's mind running, and she found herself having difficulty falling asleep.

* * * * *

The two got up the next day and got ready for the birthday party. Cathy oversaw the cake. Luckily, Cathy had already gotten a gift for both her and Kristen. And with Kristen's busy schedule, Cathy always helped pick up the slack.

Kristen stepped out in an elegant short dress.

"You look amazing!" Cathy said.

"You do as well," Kristen replied.

Cathy asked Kristen to hold the cake while she grabbed the car keys. They rode together in Cathy's vehicle since the birthday party was only a few blocks away. Kristen was worried about who all was going to be at the party.

"Do I know anyone who is coming to the party?" Kristen asked.

"You know Kim," Cathy responded. "The rest of them are very friendly."

They pulled up to the ranch-style home. Seated deep in the suburbs of Chicago, the house was in a quaint district of beautiful homes.

Cathy knocked on the front door and was greeted by Kim.

"Hey, girls!" Kim said.

Kristen was very bashful with people and especially around over-the-top extroverts like Kim. Luckily, the two had met some time before the party, and that helped alleviate the pressure on Kristen's end.

The house was full of women, and it appeared that everyone was on time. The guests were all dressed in their Sunday's finest. Kristen found her way to the hors d'oeuvres to help prevent direct communication, until she was approached by Stephanie.

"Heard you were getting married soon?" Stephanie asked.

"Yes, I am," Kristen responded.

"Enjoy it while it lasts," Stephanie said.

Kristen didn't know what to say. It was already awkward enough not knowing most anyone in the room, not to mention she already knew the situation with Stephanie's divorce.

"I'm just kidding," Stephanie responded.

"Leave her alone," Kim quickly spoke.

Stephanie quietly overlooked Kristen while Kim was trying to hold a different conversation among the group. Kristen was already stressed. She wanted to take her head and bury it in the dirt. Stephanie appeared envious of Kristen's new endeavor and life.

The doorbell rang, and Stephanie answered the door.

"Surprise!" everyone shouted in the group.

Stephanie was thrown off by the kindheartedness of her closest friends. As much as the group knew her life was in shambles, they did their best to make this moment count.

The chorus had taken off.

"Happy Birthday to you, Happy Birthday to you, Happy Birthday dear, Stephanie, Happy Birthday to you!"

Applauses echoed from around the group as Stephanie was presented by the enormous cake at her waist. The candles were like a small firepit surrounded by the sugary tower.

"Damn, I feel good!" Stephanie shouted as though it was her thank-you to the group. "I don't have to answer to anyone ever again. Life is good! No regrets!"

As the guests surrounded Stephanie and she took a huge glimpse at her cake, she paused. She couldn't hold it back. Everything that had happened to her over the past few months was weighing heavy at this moment. Not sure if it was the amount of alcohol she ingested during the party, but the tears came boldly.

"My life is such a mess!" Stephanie sobbed.

Everyone at the party was in utter silence. What could anyone say? Her life was hit by a meteor. Everything she had worked for in her marriage was gone. Not much more could be done except the empathetic hugs from everyone that huddled around her. She broke down deeply.

"Here," Kristen softly spoke as she handed Stephanie a tissue.

"Thank you," Stephanie replied as she attempted to dampen the tears.

"You can tell everyone is here for you," Kristen said. "Happy Birthday, Stephanie."

It was as though Kristen's words meant something to Stephanie. The quietest one in the group hit the highest point in Stephanie's sobbing tower of sadness. So Stephanie felt a connection with Kristen after all.

"What would you like to drink, Kristen?" Stephanie offered.

"A white wine would be great," Kristen replied.

It was as if the party had broken the mold and Kristen too. The cake was sliced without anyone getting stabbed, and the balloons and ribbons were like chandeliers hanging in the air. The women felt like sisters. What appeared abnormal for a moment was becoming a great social gathering. Sure, Stephanie was drunk, but she was in good company, which is something you couldn't buy with money.

The wine was creating an atmosphere filled with conversation. Round three and not one woman was found lying on the floor. Kristen was hitting her sweet spot with the effortless flow of bubbly. Then the crowd turned to her and asked what Cathy had been telling them all along.

"We heard you have an interesting story to tell, Kristen," said the group.

Kristen felt awkward in a way, but the wine kept her from holding back.

"Sure," Kristen replied. "Let me tell you about a story of a man I met on the subway."

The whole group was slouched on the living room furniture as Kristen started to open up.

* * * * *

After getting off the subway one day, Kristen noticed a homeless man sitting in the corner at the bottom of the stairs. He was playing cards as he gently asked her a question.

"Do you have any spare change to offer, ma'am?" he asked.

Kristen felt sorry for the man and gave him a couple of dollars.

He had a beard and appeared a little rugged. He had tattoos covering his forearms and long hair that reached the midpart of his back. He thanked her for the couple of spare dollars she had in her purse.

"God bless you," he continued.

* * * * *

Kristen let the group know that this one act of kindness became a habit for her. Every time she came across someone in need, Kristen gave what she could in the moment.

* * * * *

One particular day, Kristen was meditating on a project she needed to present to her boss the following day.

The homeless man stuck out his hand again, but Kristen told him that she didn't have any spare change that day.

He said, "Don't worry, ma'am. I know you have a big heart for helping others. I can see it."

Kristen found a seat where she was going over her project when she noticed two men who were sitting next to her. They started scooting their way toward her. They began harassing me with derogatory comments and made her feel very uncomfortable.

Watching in the distance was the homeless man. He saw what was happening and began walking toward the men.

"Leave her alone!" he shouted. "Otherwise, I'm going to have to hurt you."

The men could tell this homeless man meant business as he had his hand wrapped around a switchblade on his right side.

The men slowly got up and backstepped their way out of sight. Kristen couldn't believe her eyes. It was like this man was her saving grace. She thanked him for helping her, and he gently smiled as if it was no problem at all.

"I will sit next to you until the next train stop, if you don't mind, ma'am?" he kindly suggested.

Kristen didn't mind as he basically saved her life. She felt like she owed him something more than money. Maybe an ear was all he needed.

"What's your name?" Kristen asked.

"My name?" he replied. "It's John."

"Very nice to meet you, John," Kristen said.

Through their conversation over the next few minutes, Kristen found out that John was a veteran. Kristen wondered what happened to him and how he had gone from being veteran to a homeless man without any possessions.

"It's a long story," John said.

The subway was coming to a halt, and Kristen had to get off the train, which interrupted their conversation.

"Well, this is my stop," Kristen said, "But thank you again, John."

As the weeks went by, Kristen found John at the same spot—at the bottom of the stairs on the subway, playing his usual game of cards and asking for spare change. John did not appear to be the type of person who had an addiction, always asking for money to get his next "fix." Instead, he always appeared to be genuine, and quite reserved, to say the least.

Kristen developed a relationship with John. And she became curious about his past. One day, Kristen got the courage to ask John about his previous life.

"Do you mind telling me your story, John?" Kristen asked.

"Are you sure you have time to listen?" John spoke.

"I do, John," Kristen replied.

John, at one point in time was married many years ago. He told Kristen about a daughter he had, who he'd never known. He opened up and talked about how much the Iraq War had brought a lot of turmoil to his life. He was an alcoholic upon returning home, and his marriage fell apart.

John continued to tell Kristen that he had difficulty concentrating on his family's needs. He just couldn't stay focused on the love he wanted to share with them, the time he wanted to spend with them, and the hands-on father figure he wanted to be for his daughter. Unfortunately, to make things worse, his wife was diagnosed with breast cancer, and so he ran.

John's alcohol problem worsened, and he was suffering from severe depression and PTSD. He failed to receive treatment from the Veteran's Association, and this left John in the predicament he was in now. It was a slippery slope from which he never recovered.

John lost everything and ended up on the streets of Chicago. John started to cry. John told Kristen how much he loved his family, but that he was a coward and ran from his problems. He didn't even know if his wife was still alive or if his daughter was okay. He just ran as fast as he could.

Over the years, John vowed to stay clean after he found himself in and out of jail, along with a mudslide of tickets he owed to the city. He thought that if there were one thing he could give his absent family, it was the gift to stay clean.

"I still to this day don't know where my daughter is," John spoke. "She will be roughly twenty-something years old this year."

John had trouble with memory. And for the life of him, dates, times, and details were a hard thing to grasp. His past military trauma played a role in what he is struggling with today.

John told Kristen that he used to write poems for his daughter, Samantha, and kept them tucked away in his knapsack.

John said, "My daughter was four years old when I left the home." He wrote so many apology letters that he started to overlap them, which provoked him to throw many of them away. Again, John started to cry as the memories came flooding back.

Kristen felt empathy for John. She wondered what it was like to live in his world. The two of them were living contrasted lives. Kristen was a successful businesswoman, and John didn't have a pot to piss in, as all seemed lost. It amazed her how the two were joined in conversation and yet separated in livelihood.

Then it hit her.

"Oh my gosh, John!" Kristen squealed. "What if I published one of your poems in the *Chicago Tribune*?"

John lifted his head in excitement and attempted to grasp what Kristen was saying.

"It's possible your daughter or wife might see the column and contact me." Kristen was like a child with the flights of ideas she was having. Kristen felt like her purpose was to connect this man back to his daughter!

Chapter

4

The entire group at Stephanie's birthday was sitting on the edge of their seats.

Kristen's personality started to come out, and she was her old, bubbling self again. The girls at the birthday party were so inspired by Kristen's story that they hardly took any sips of their wine. Let's be honest, some of them could hardly hold their heads up from all the liquor they had ingested.

Kristen had done it. She decided to gamble on John's story and get his poems into the *Chicago Tribune*. Everything she had strived for in life was summed up in this one goal—to find John's daughter again!

Over the next few days, Kristen accumulated all the poems that John had held dearly to his heart. They were crumbled and mildly stained but good enough to read. They might have smelled a little too, but Kristen looked past the hygiene criteria and presented them to the *Chicago Tribune*. And wouldn't you know it, they published the poems along with a cover story!

The response was big.

People from all over the city fell in love with John's writings. You could tell they were written by a father who dearly adored his long-lost daughter. The readers could tell by the tangible verbiage that John was expressing himself, both in heartache and in joy.

Word was getting out about John's poems over the next few weeks as more newspapers hit the shelves. Some of the titles of these cover stories included "A Father Looking for Hope," "A Daughter

He Never Knew," and "Homeless but Still Hopeful." John was even impressed by the titles.

John and Kristen became best friends as they chuckled together under the awning on the Chicago streets. Kristen made every effort to meet with John once a new story came out. John was bashful about what the writers were saying because he was never the popular type. Nevertheless, John accepted this as a blessing and waited every day for his daughter to call him.

Over the weeks, however, there were no phone calls. On the contrary, John was getting a lot of admirers who wanted to meet him and give him money. This was not the result John wanted. He hoped for the warm touch of his daughter's hand caressing his. You see, John was after the physical presence of his daughter, not the glamour of a fan fluffing up his ego.

Kristen found herself bewildered. And for some odd reason, she felt like everything was right—the right newspaper, the right content, and the right person. But what she found herself drawing up a fan base of wild women wanting the delicate John who they could take home as a pet. This did not sit well with Kristen.

"I'm so sorry, John," Kristen said.

"What do you mean?" John replied.

"This has turned into a circus side show, and you were never intended to be the attraction," Kristen continued. "I thought that broadcasting these poems would bring your daughter home. Unfortunately, they haven't done so yet."

"Oh, Kristen, my dear, it's not your fault. You tried," John replied.

John didn't have high hopes in life, so something like this didn't chaff his mood. He thought if it was intended to be, it would happen. Kristen, on the other hand, kept her frustration bottled up inside.

* * * * *

Kristen gets a call from the *Chicago Tribune* that someone is looking for the author of the poems. She was in shock and excited to hear this news. The following day she tells John about this good news.

"Thank you, Kristen, for everything," John exclaimed excitedly. John was out of this world hearing the news. "So when can I see her?" John asked.

Kristen tells him that she is going to talk to her and arrange the meeting soon.

Kristen calls the number given to her by the *Chicago Tribune*.

"Hello, can I speak to Samantha?" Kristen asked.

"This is Samantha," the lady replied.

"I'm the person who published the poems in the *Chicago Tribune*," Kristen stated.

Samantha asked Kristen where she found these poems. Kristen says that someone at the subway station gave them to her to get them published. Kristen didn't want to reveal that the person is homeless yet.

"I would like to meet him," Samantha insisted.

"Sure," Kristen agreed. "Let me know when you would like to meet him."

"I live in Madison, Wisconsin," Samantha said. "How about this coming Friday? I can come to Chicago."

"That's great, Samantha," Kristen replied. "How about I meet you at six p.m. at the subway area."

"That's sounds great," Samantha assured. "Thank you, Kristen, for helping me get to meet my dad. I appreciate it."

Kristen shared this information with John.

Hearing this, John started tearing. Stammering, John said, "Kristen, you are amazing. I don't know how to thank you."

"You don't have to," Kristen replied.

Kristen arrived at the subway station at 6:00 p.m. Samantha called Kristen, saying that she would be there in fifteen minutes. Kristen started looking for John at his usual place. She was little nervous at not seeing him. Her heart was pounding fast.

"Did something happen with him last night? How will I answer to Samantha?"

Someone called out Kristen's name. She turned back and saw a middle-aged person who was dressed well. It was a handsome man wearing sunglasses. She was surprised that this man knew her name.

"Kristen, it's me," John said.

"Oh, my gosh," Kristen said in amazement. "What were all those days when I saw you as a homeless man?"

"I will explain more later," John stated. "I was an undercover police officer until yesterday. After getting cleaned up, I joined the Chicago Police Department with the help of my Iraq veteran friend. Given my military background, getting trained as a police officer was a little easier."

"Wow, John, you are amazing," Kristen said. "I'm happy for you."

"Kristen, I'm getting a call," John said. "It's Samantha."

Kristen told John to wait, and she went up the stairs to meet Samantha.

"You must be Kristen?" Samantha questioned.

Kristen and Samantha then walked down the stairs to meet John.

John was eagerly waiting to meet his daughter after so many years. His heart was pounding, and his hands were soaked with sweat. Kristen introduces Samantha to John. Samantha didn't recognize John. She remembered her father as being taller and heftier. She asked John his last name. He told her it's Hester.

"Sorry, my dad's last name is Smith," Samantha said.

Then John remembered that Samantha is the daughter of his Iraqi war buddy. They both were very close and shared many things, including the poems. John realized that his war buddy, Mr. Smith, might have recited the poems to Samantha when she was young.

"I'm sorry to hear that you're also looking for your dad."

While John was obviously disappointed, he was still happy see his buddy's daughter.

"I will contact you if I hear anything about your dad," John promised Samantha.

"I really appreciate it, John," Samantha said graciously.

"Sorry I disappointed you, Samantha," John said.

"No, John, not at all," Samantha assured. "I'm happy to see my dad's best friend."

Kristen was a little disappointed, but she recovered fast, hearing these kind words from John. And John was still so grateful to Kristen.

"I don't know how I can thank you enough you're your kindness," John emphasized.

Kristen smiled.

"We will keep in touch, Samantha," John states. "Have a safe trip back to Madison."

Kristen told John that she strongly believe she is going to find his wife and daughter soon.

"Thank you, Kristen," John said. "Here is my card. Please don't hesitate to call me if you need any help."

"Thank you, John," Kristen replied.

* * * * *

Everyone at the party was holding their breath at this moment. Hearing this story about Kristen really opened their eyes to her caring nature. She was like a mother hen looking over her chick. Kristen had a heart the size of Chicago's famous public Cloud Gate monument, something no one could bypass.

"Wow!" shouted one of the girls. "You really are right, every homeless person has a story to tell. Well, that day is not far away, with John meeting his daughter. I truly believe and wish that it's going to happen. John will meet his daughter. And, Kristen, won't forget to let us know when that happens. We all pray that John will find his daughter and wife soon."

"Me too," said Kristen with a big smile.

* * * * * *

Kristen found herself in a moment of reliving her memories. The childhood she grew up in, not having a father figure around. Kristen wondered what it was like for John's daughter, whom he never knew. She wondered about the vacancy in both her heart and

27

John's. Life, for Kristen, was good. But there was still an empty childhood somewhere in her own life that she still recalled.

As Kristen was sitting there in her thoughts, everyone at the party turned to the clock.

"Shoot, it's already ten p.m." One of the girls brought the time to everyone's attention.

Suddenly, Kristen's silenced thoughts brought her back to reality, and she helped get things cleaned up at the party before she and Cathy headed out the door.

Both Kristen and Cathy got into the car and drove off through the city.

Kristen's eyes were on the illuminating lights panning across her window. The emotions she had running through her mind were evolving. How simple life would be if she didn't have a care in the world. However, her thoughts became like daggers, as she tried to accumulate some sort of childhood memory of her father growing up.

Kristen always hid her emotions in front of others. But with Cathy, they just spilled out.

"Are you okay, Kristen?" Cathy asked from the driver's seat.

"I'll be fine, Cathy," Kristen replied.

"You don't look okay," Cathy stated.

"Just thinking about life and the details of it," Kristen replied.

"Listen, I know you don't know your father," Cathy said. "But maybe one day you'll finally meet him."

"That day may come, Cathy," Kristen replied. "Just not today."

Cathy was concerned for Kristen. They could talk about anything, except for Kristen's father. That was something Kristen held deep down in the trough of her emotions, a deep well of unknowing. And for whatever reason, Cathy was okay not knowing everything about Kristen's past, so she always seemed to focus more on the positive.

* * * * *

The alarm went off the next morning.

Kristen reached over to turn off the bellow of noise screeching from her alarm. She stretched as if she'd overused her entire body the night before. Kristen's life had become so routine since moving to Chicago. Daily life was like a machine. Everyone in the city was running, not knowing where they were headed. Sure, they had their jobs, but life itself was mechanical, going nowhere.

Kristen noticed that in the big city no one even has time to look around. And with the drowning of cell phones, music, and daily tabloids, people succumbed to life in the fast lane.

Kristen wondered to herself, *Maybe this is who I have become among them. A casualty to a life of business with no real direction or purpose.* These thoughts were daunting to Kristen.

Kirsten grew up a free bird, living in Potomac, and enjoying many simple things: riding horses, chasing her dogs, nature, and the driven community that was so closely knit together. Everyone knew everyone in this small town. The city, however, rarely engaged in conversation. The people of Potomac helped one another. Kristen's values guided her into the woman she is today.

Kristen hightailed it to the train station.

Temperatures that morning were in the midforties. Kristen was walking at a fast pace to meet her departure. Luckily, she entered the doors at the last minute and quietly took her seat so as not to draw attention to herself. Kristen looked to an admirer sitting right next to her and gave a bit of a side smile. It was an older woman was sitting to her left.

"Oh my, look at you," the older woman stated. "Why are you so beautiful?"

"Thank you," Kristen replied as she blushed.

"The guy who marries you is one lucky guy," the older woman continued.

"Actually, I'm engaged," Kristen replied.

Then Kristen drew out her hand to show the woman her ring and the people around them were also interested.

"Congratulations!" the older woman shouted. "You know, I got married when I was twenty-five years old. I dated my husband for two years before we got married."

Kristen was engaging in conversation with this woman as if she held the wisdom to life.

"Did you say yes right away?" the older woman asked.

"Well…yes, yes, I did," Kristen answered. "It was the best day of my life."

The two chuckled as if they unconsciously knew what each other thought about the best day of each other's lives. Women are giddy over a good romance story.

The two continued their conversation as the older woman talked about her most memorable moments of being married. They were married for more than fifty years. Not that they didn't have their ups and downs; but that life together, through trust and commitment, was their bond for one another.

Kristen was inspired by their long legacy and commitment of marriage. She dreamed that her and Michael had the same grace to foolishly stay in love throughout their years together. Kristen was the committed type. When she put her head to something, it stuck.

The older woman went on to tell Kristen that she lost her husband one year ago to a heart attack. You could see the loss of a loved one through the lens of her eyes. But the story of Kristen's engagement brought hope back into the woman's life that love still existed.

"Well, I wish you both well in life," the older woman announced. "This is my next stop."

"It was such a pleasure meeting you," Kristen said.

"Likewise," the older woman said. "You have a good day."

Kristen was encouraged by the older woman's story. In fact, it pushed her to recall all the moments leading up to her engagement. The dinner adventures, the long conversations, Michael in rare form and his charismatic personality, with each memory leading all the way up to her engagement when she said, "I will."

The train was cruising through the city as the skyscrapers emerged into her view. The Sears Tower stood out, reaching to the clouds in the sky and resembling the beanstalk in *Jack and the Beanstalk*. Lake Michigan was a cool blue that would catch your eyes as the sun reflected off the surface of the water. Chicago was not so bad at all. Kristen did, however, realize that she missed her hometown and the people there and especially her mom. Kristen's mom took care of everything and never once did she yell when Kristen was wrong.

As Kristen got off the train, she was overtaken by the scene in front of her. Three police officers, out of nowhere, chased a man who had been caught stealing from a nearby convenient store. They subdued the man and handcuffed him. This was normal to Kristen now. She had become accustomed to the spontaneous crimes happening and all the overbearing downtown noises.

Kristen stayed with her routine. She noticed a homeless man on the sidewalk and gave the normal spare change that was always available deep in her purse.

Kristen made it to work on time. But she had to play a little catch-up. She called the printing press where her wedding cards were being made. They were done and ready to be picked up at 7:00 p.m. that night.

* * * * *

The day went by so fast. Before Kristen knew it, it was time to leave work. She took the train back home and made it to her apartment. Slumped down to indulge in her wind-down Coca-Cola, she almost forgot about picking up the wedding invitations. She dashed over to pick up Cathy's keys and hurried out the door.

Kristen's mind was running as fast as the lights were panning over her car. She made it to the printing store at 6:30 p.m., just before it closed.

"Here are your wedding invitations," the teller stated.

Kristen opened the envelope to check for mistakes. Everything looked good.

Kristen paid the woman and jumped back into the car to head home. Kristen was so overjoyed knowing that she was getting married in just a few weeks. The invitations opened her eyes and reality was setting in now.

She buckled herself in the car and drove toward the main road. Kristen was thinking too many things all at one time. She sat at the stop light, waiting for the light to turn green.

She took her foot off the brake once the light turned green and merged onto the intersection. As her vehicle made its way into the center intersection, suddenly, a truck's lights came quickly into Kristen's view. She didn't even have time to react.

Kristen was paralyzed by the truck's headlights as they came dashing into her driver's side, striking with force. The car, pushed from its forward motion, began to tumble, rolling over and over to the side of the road. The crashing sound could have awakened residents from five blocks in all different directions. Glass was shattered like crystal diamonds all over the pavement. Her driver's door was caved in, like a sheet of paper and crumbled to nothing.

Wedding cards floated in the air and across the plain of the street. It was like her entire life just took a turn for the worse. She tried to grip anything she could find as the turning of her vehicle continued, seeming never to stop. Finally, the car came to a stop; the wheels now back on the ground.

Kristen couldn't think of anything besides the excruciating pain coming from her right hip. She could vaguely saw several civilians in the distance rushing toward her vehicle.

"Are you okay?" shouted one of the civilians in the distance.

"I'm hurting. Someone please call 911," Kristen struggled.

"Help is on the way," they responded.

Kristen was looking down at her lap. She could see the streams of blood coming from her body. The car was destroyed. Her life, for where it was now, appeared to be in shambles; and she didn't have time to think about everyone else and how they would be impacted by this wreck.

A few minutes had passed, and the police lights flickered in the distance. Sirens on the ambulance followed the red and blue lights.

Kristen was beginning to feel dizzy and nauseous, like she was going to vomit. Someone reached across Kristen's seat and unbuckled her. Luckily, Kristen was buckled in, or she would have likely been ejected and not lived.

The paramedics carried Kristen slowly out of the vehicle and onto a stretcher. Quickly, they placed a c-collar around her neck for support. Kristen's pulse, however, was weak, like she might be losing blood internally. Her blood pressure was low. The paramedics placed a couple IVs in her for stability. Kristen was in bad shape.

As the ambulance hightailed it toward the hospital, they made a call to the charge nurse in the ER. They received orders to give Kristen boluses of normal saline to keep her pressure up. She was conscious. Overwhelmed by the pain, Kristen was coming back to her senses.

"I don't know what happened," Kristen spoke softly. "I think I got T-boned. Is the truck driver, okay?"

"We think so ma'am," the paramedic responded. "There were a few minor injuries, but he should be okay. The police are looking into the accident. Do you have any pain?"

"Yes, my right hip, belly, and thigh," Kristen responded. "I think I lost my phone back at the accident. Will you call my fiancé?"

"Sure thing, once we get to the hospital," the paramedic responded.

The ambulance reached Northwestern Hospital in Chicago. The paramedics called Michael on their phone before the ER staff approached the vehicle.

"Hello, Michael?" Kristen spoke. "I'm here at the hospital. I was injured badly in a wreck."

"Oh my gosh, Kristen," Michael quickly responded. "What happened?"

"I'll explain everything later," Kristen replied. "I'm here at Northwestern Hospital."

"I'm on my way," Michael responded.

"Okay, I love you," Kristen closed the conversation.

The ER trauma team rushed to the ambulance doors to greet Kristen. They moved her into the trauma bay in the emergency department to check her labs, get X-rays of her hip and extremities, and a CT scan of her abdomen.

"Hello, Kristen, I'm trauma surgeon Akpanuno."

Kristen glanced at the surgeon through the dried blood in her hair and some minor cuts on her face. The staff ran into the room to give the surgeon her critical lab.

"Sir, her hemoglobin is five grams."

"Okay we will need to transfuse three units of blood now!" Then the surgeon glanced back at Kristen to tell her everything was going to be all right.

The X-rays that came back showed a femur fracture, which was the reason for Kristen's right hip pain. They quickly transfused three units of blood and were bringing Kristen's blood pressure back to normal. The CT scan, however, showed that she was bleeding internally into her peritoneum and needed exploratory surgery to find the bleeding.

The OR was called and given an update with orders to prep for surgery. Michael had still not arrived at this point. Kristen was terrified. Everything was moving at such a rapid pace, and Kristen didn't know if her life was in danger or not. She just had to trust the hospital staff and their professionalism.

Finally, the OR was prepped and ready. Kristen was given IV analgesics and sedation. She started to feel drowsy. She mumbled to the staff to tell Michael she loved him. Kristen's blood pressure started to plummet again. They desperately needed to get her to surgery, or she could die. They were pumping Kristen full of fluids and plasma to help sustain her pressure.

They moved Kristen into the operating suite. She was prepped for surgery and was tubed to stabilize her breathing during surgery. The trauma surgeon made an incision with no further delay. The whole peritoneal cavity was filled with blood. They had to suction a lot of blood from Kristen's belly. The surgeon noticed the blood was traced all the way toward her uterus. It appeared that Kristen had an avulsion from her seatbelt injury. They had to immediately call the obstetrics surgeon in the hospital as this was a case beyond his specialty.

The OB surgeon was paged and ran immediately to the operating room. Once the surgeon was updated and exploration was done, she noticed the uterus was lacerated badly. Being so young, the surgeon wanted to save Kristen's uterus. It could potentially need to be surgically removed if not fixed. Luckily, she was successful in repairing the uterus and controlling the bleeding.

Immediately, Kristen's blood pressure started coming up. She was being stabilized. The repair of the uterus was the culprit for her blood loss. Everything seemed as though it was going to be okay.

*   *   *   *   *

After surgery, they moved Kristen to post-op where she would be considered in stable condition. By now, Michael had reached the hospital and was pacing in the waiting room to get an update on Kristen. They finally allowed Michael to see her. He couldn't believe Kristen's condition.

"Hey, honey," Michael softly said.

"Hi, Michael," Kristen responded.

Tears were running down Kristen's face. She didn't know if it was her adrenaline catching back up or the fact that Michael was seeing her in such a difficult condition. The OB surgeon arrived in the room to provide an update. The surgeon took a deep breath before explaining the incident.

"The surgery was successful. We were able to control your bleeding once we found out you had a uterus laceration that was bleeding profusely from the inside. There was a benign growth on the uterus that appeared to be pushing on the point where you had the seatbelt injury. Anyway, I believe you will still be able to have children once you recover."

Kristen and Michael were sitting with hands held tight, nodding to the surgeon. Once the surgeon left the room, Michael started asking what happened. Kristen let him know that she believes she'd been T-boned on the driver's side. Everything happened so fast that it was hard for her to grasp the entirety of the accident, but she did the best she could.

The trauma surgeon entered the room next.

"Hello guys," the surgeon spoke. "How are you feeling?"

"I still have pain in my right side," Kristen responded.

"You have a femur fracture that will need surgery in a couple days once the swelling goes down," the surgeon stated. "You had a small laceration to your face that we sutured as well."

"How long will I be in the hospital?" Kristen asked.

"Let's see in the coming days. You just get some rest for now," the surgeon replied.

"Thank you doctor," Kristen replied.

"I'll keep you updated," the surgeon closed.

Kristen's face was swollen like a saturated watermelon. She asked Michael if he had called her mother.

"Not yet," Michael replied.

"Please let her know the situation and that surgery went okay," Kristen responded.

Michael made his way out of the room and into the lobby to call Kristen's mom.

Kristen's mother picked up.

"Hello," Michael spoke. "It's Michael."

"Yes, Michael?" Kristen's mother responded.

"I'm calling to let you know that Kristen was involved in a wreck," Michael stated.

"Oh my gosh!" Kristen's mother shouted. "Is she okay?"

"She is now," Michael responded. "She's out of surgery and doing well."

Kristen's mother had to sit down. Overwhelmed by the news, she didn't have much to say after that except getting in her car and driving to the hospital.

"I'll be there by tonight," Kristen's mother stated.

"Sure," Michael responded. "We're here at Northwestern Hospital."

"See you in a bit," Kristen's mother replied.

* * * * *

Kristen was finally moved to her regular room for hospital admission. She had IVs in both of her arms, a splint stationed over her right leg, and aches and pains she never felt before. Kristen was stable but had a long road of recovery ahead of her.

Outside in the hospital lobby, Michael's parents had showed up. Not for support, more so to give Michael a reality check.

"Are you crazy, Michael, you're still wanting to marry her?" Michael's dad announced. "Our family legacy will end with you."

The harsh words coming from Michael's dad's lips didn't settle well with Michael. He always thought highly of his father's remarks, good or bad.

"We just think you should make the right decision here, Michael," Michael's mother spoke.

Unfortunately, this conversation was heard by Kristen in the distance. She felt belittled, like an abandoned child whose parents don't want her. It could have been from the amount of pain medication she was on now, but nevertheless, Kristen was still emotional.

Michael's parents walked uncomfortably into Kristen's room to check up on her. Kristen was dozing in and out due to her pain medication.

"Let's let her sleep," Michael told his parents. "She has a long road of recovery ahead of her."

* * * * * *

Over the next couple of days, Kristen was pumped full of IV antibiotics. The staff at the hospital was so kind and compassionate in caring for her, and she felt the warm comfort of their presence. However, Kristen's emotions were unstable because of the nature of her situation. One evening she woke up out of a dead sleep sobbing.

"I don't think I will be ready for my wedding in a few short weeks," Kristen cried.

A nurse rushed into the room as she heard Kristen sobbing from a distance. She sat down to hold Kristen's hand. Questions popped into Kristen's mind.

Will Michael walk away from the wedding? Will his parents even accept me as a daughter-in-law? So many things…

"Everything will be all right," the nurse spoke.

"Thank you so much," Kristen responded.

Kristen was a wreck, not just physically but emotionally as well. Everything from the preparation for the wedding to an unfortunate circumstance that has now left everything stationary, Kristen felt even more overwhelmed now than she did prior to the wreck. She wondered about her physical well-being and whether she'd even be able to walk down the aisle or not. How far they were going to have to push the wedding out and reset everything again. It was certain that Kristen was having her doubts. Somewhere deep inside her heart, Kristen felt this uncomfortable feeling that Michael would leave her.

He seemed checked-out by his body language. She wasn't sure if it was Michael's parents that were provoking him to call off the wedding or his shortness in his conversations with her. Not to mention, he didn't seem to visit her in the hospital nearly as much as she had hoped. She knew that Michael still had work to do, but you put your regularly scheduled life on hold for something this important. At least, that's what Kristen thought Michael should do.

Chapter

6

Kristen had recovered enough in her regular room that she was now ready for surgery. Her right femur and right radius were both badly fractured. Once the swelling subsided, the orthopedic surgeon felt she would do well.

They prepped Kristen for surgery, she signed her consent forms, and it was off to surgery in the operating room. Kristen noticed the flashing lights overhead that panned across her view as she was lying in a supine position. Kristen felt the warmth of the health-care workers who were there to make sure she had the best care possible. It felt weird though, Michael was nowhere to be found prior to surgery.

The medications flowed through Kristen's IV, and she slowly fell asleep from the anesthesia, as she looked at the masked faces looking over her with reassurances that everything would be all right.

* * * *

The surgery took hours. Kristen had a femur neck fracture that took precise screws and pinning to help stabilize her hip. In addition to all that, Kristen had a radial head prosthesis fitted so that she could reuse her arm again. Both surgeries went better than expected. Kristen didn't lose any blood during the process, and the fastening of the fractures easily lined up.

Once the surgery was completed, the team moved Kristen back to recovery, where she had ice chips and postoperative analgesics.

Surprisingly, Kristen felt good. Her mindset was focused on recovery. The nurses caring for Kristen waited on her hand and foot and thanked them for every answered call.

Now that Kristen's hip and arm were fixed, the physicians felt it would be best to move her to a skilled nursing facility for rehabilitation, both for physical and occupational therapy. This would help Kristen get better use of her arm and leg. So she agreed with the orders and was placed in a skilled nursing facility not far from the hospital.

The skilled nursing facility was an above-the-norm type of place. This place was a gem and not at all like your typical nursing home. Donned with fresh paint, modern furniture, and spacious rooms, Kristen didn't know if she would even want to leave this place and move back to her apartment with Cathy. All jokes aside, Kristen was gracious to be in such a beautiful facility.

Over the next several days, life wasn't any easier. The pain was excruciating. Kristen felt sharp, throbbing pain coming from her hip. Physical therapy only made things worse, although Kristen had been told it was going to be tough at first but would improve over time. Nevertheless, the pain seemed to always stay at the forefront of Kristen's mind.

She was given oral analgesics that helped with the pain, but she never took it. As the days progressed into weeks, there was still no sign of Michael. Kristen tried calling but did not received an answer. She left countless voice messages for him to reach her at the skilled nursing facility as Kristen had lost her cell phone in the wreck.

Nothing happened. It was like Michael had abandoned her. Sure, he was there initially after the wreck, but overtime, Michael's presence lessened and lessened until there was no sign of him at all. Not only was Kristen's wedding approaching, but the groom to garnish the wedding was nowhere to be found. Cathy couldn't find him. Kristen's mother couldn't find him. All hope seemed lost.

One day, out of the blue though, Kristen received some peculiar mail. It was from Michael.

Kristen quickly opened the envelope and pulled out the short letter. This is what Michael wrote:

Kristen,

> *What can I say? This has been a hard journey for both of us. What we have is something special, and I knew that. But overtime it appears that we have drifted apart, and now I'm questioning the future of our lives. Do I love you? Of course. Do I want the best for you? More than anything. That is why I am writing this letter to you now. Kristen, I want what is best for you, and I don't think that's me. I have grappled with these thoughts for some time now, and for the life of me, they can't escape my mind. So I want to let you know, I'm calling off the wedding. I think it's best we both move on with our lives and love each other the best way we know how. I'm sorry you are getting this news through a letter and not in person. As much as I would like that, I feel it would make it harder on the both of us. I'm leaving Chicago. I have accepted a job position in Seattle, and I'm moving next week. What we had was love, but I believe I love you more by saying farewell. To the woman who helped shape my life. I love you.*

> *Michael*

Kristen felt pain as if someone had stabbed her in the heart, and she cried. Okay, she was wailing so much that everyone down the hallway stepped out of their rooms to see what all the commotion was about. Kristen felt betrayed. She felt confused. She tore the letter into a million pieces. And then the pieces that were left, Kristen dropped into a trash can next to her bed.

Kristen gripped her hip as the wailing cries exacerbated the pain she felt. She called for the nurse. The nurses came storming into the room to see what had happened. They thought Kristen had fallen out of bed with all the loud cries coming from her room. She asked for more pain medication. And they gladly gave her a dose to help mend the sorrow.

As the nurses left the room, a woman entered. She was an older woman, no more than seventy years old. She had the perfect perm and the most charismatic eyes. It was dark in the doorway, so it was difficult for Kristen to make out the woman's silhouette. But when the woman approached the bed, Kristen saw her physical features. Her name was Margaret.

"Are you okay, my dear?" Margaret questioned.

Kristen could barely speak through the tears that filled her eyes. She was sniffling, gasping, and attempting to keep her composure. But she felt like her heart had been torn from her torso. Margaret showed her compassion by handing Kristen a Kleenex.

Kristen had to blow the slimy snot accumulated from her outbreak of cries. But she was slowly bringing it back together.

"Thank you so much," Kristen voiced.

"What happened?" Margaret asked.

"Well...I just found out my fiancé dumped me," Kristen sobbed. "And through a letter!"

"That's shallow, my dear," Margaret announced.

"That's what I thought!" Kristen shouted.

"You'll find you a good man one day, my dear," Margaret stated. "When I was younger, I had many men who I dumped."

"Men you dumped?" Kristen questioned.

"Oh yes, my dear," Margaret responded. "You dump them before they dump you."

Kristen burst out into a bellowing laugh. Whatever she was enduring, Margaret seemed to break the seal with her humor. She could tell Margaret was a jokester, someone that Kristen desperately needed right now to help make her laugh through this current situation.

Margaret became Kristen's saving grace. Everyday Margaret would show up to listen and help humor Kristen back to recovery. Margaret helped tuck Kristen into bed. And Margaret helped cut Kristen's meals, even though she "soured" over the food there. Margaret always found time to graze the vending machines instead of eating the "poison" being served at this facility.

In the same instance, Margaret was falling in love with Kristen. You see, Margaret lost her daughter in an accident when she was twenty-six years old. Kristen strongly reminded Margaret of her daughter. This only made their relationship with each other even stronger.

Margaret was in this facility because of some generalized weakness she had endured a couple weeks prior to Kristen's arrival and needed to improve her strength. Margaret happened to be a very wealthy woman. You could tell by her hair and jewelry that she was serious. Before walking out of her room, Margaret always made sure she was dressed to the gills.

One day, while visiting Margaret in her room, a man gently walked in behind Kristen.

"Well, hello, my dear," Margaret announced. "Come in, come in."

His name was Louis Foster. He wore a long, wool overcoat. His hair was stylish and perhaps a look Tom Cruise would appreciate. He was handsome, tall, had a great physique. He was eye-catching to Kristen. She was almost embarrassed to be sitting in a wheelchair with the looks of this man in front of her.

Foster introduced himself as a consultant for a financial company. Nothing that he gloated about, but you could tell he was proud about it.

Kristen suddenly had a phone call from her room. It was the insurance company involved with her wreck.

"May I speak with Kristen, please," the insurance agent announced.

"This is she," Kristen responded.

"Yes, ma'am, I have a few questions for you," the agent stated.

"Sure, go ahead," Kristen responded.

"Do you feel that you crossed the red light accidently?" the agent questioned.

"No," Kristen responded.

"There were eyewitnesses at the scene that say you did," the agent stated.

"Yes, but the police report has evidence that says otherwise," Kristen responded.

Suddenly, Kristen started feeling agonizing pain in her hip again. She had to put down the phone. Foster heard her cries and entered the room. He could tell Kristen was still on the phone with someone.

"Hello?" Foster answered.

"Yes, this is Agent Keller with Kristen's insurance company," the agent responded. "There are allegations that Kristen is at fault in this matter."

"Okay, you will have to take that up with her lawyer," Foster announced.

"But I don't have a lawyer," Kristen abruptly spoke.

"Well, you do now," Foster stated. "He will call your insurance company tomorrow."

"Okay, thank you, sir," the agent responded.

Foster then quickly hung up the phone. He began to tell Kristen that he has a buddy who is a good lawyer and will take her case. Kristen was worried about the cost. Foster told her confidently not to worry about it. Kristen felt the warmth of Foster's words bundle her. She felt comfort in Foster's confidence.

"I hope I'm not bothering you?" Foster asked.

"No, not at all," Kristen responded. "Thank you."

"Pleasure is mine," Foster said.

"I love your aunt Margaret," Kristen voiced. "She has done nothing but help me during this circumstance."

Foster then opened up about his history with Margaret. How she raised him from when he was five to twelve years old. Foster remembered how he used to call her Mom. She has always been the kind, loving, awesome woman that she still is today. Kristen appreciated Foster's kind words toward this woman, especially her beloved friend.

"I came here to take my aunt Margaret out, but she told me she's too tired," Foster said. "Instead, she asked me to take you out."

Kristen paused in excitement.

"Maybe when you feel better, I will take you out to Lake Michigan?" Foster asked.

"I would like that," Kristen answered.

There was something in the air that day. Kristen and Foster could both sense it. Through the pain, betrayal, and uncertainty, Kristen was seeing light once again. The road ahead was difficult, but Kristen knew that through the hearts of others who shared their lives with her, she could overcome any battle or loss that came her way.

It appeared that Kristen's life was taking another turn for the better. And it would come when Kristen least expected it. Through the heartbreak of one comes the open invitation to finding true love once again. It would begin by finding a new path. And Louis Foster would be that path toward happiness once again.

Chapter 7

Kristen was overtaken by Foster's confident and charismatic nature. This is something she had seen in Michael, but Foster carried a different compassion that she'd not seen before. The days grew shorter as Kristen anticipated Foster coming to the skilled nursing facility every day. She thought about him, not just in person but when he was not there as well.

The two shaped a perfect friendship. Foster would wheel Kristen out to the Lakeshore Garden Place in a hospital van. Pushing her in a wheelchair and displaying his spontaneous heart, Foster showed Kristen all the beauty of the decorative flowers. In fact, flowers became a common display of Foster's affection for Kristen.

They would show up on Kristen's table in her room. Therapists were overtaken by the splendor of assorted colors, giving Kristen assurance of the beautiful bouquets. Kristen was embarrassed by the generosity of Foster's continuous gift of flower arrangements he gave without asking her. Nevertheless, she felt love again.

* * * * *

Kristen decided she'd call Foster one afternoon after receiving such a beautiful bouquet. She looked for the phone number that Foster gave to her during his initial visit. Once she had the phone number, she called Foster's office. His secretary answered the phone and asked who Kristen wanted.

"Ma'am, this is Kristen, a friend of Foster."

Foster gave instructions to his secretary to interrupt him, even if he's in a meeting, should he get a call from Kristen.

Foster's secretary asked him, "Who is this person you are asking for specifically?"

But Foster just smiled and said nothing. However, Foster's secretary told him she got it.

"Please hold for a second," Foster's secretary told Kristen. "He will be with you in a moment."

"I will speak to him later if he is busy," Kristen spoke.

"He is free now anyway," Foster's secretary said.

"Thank you, ma'am," Kristen politely said.

"Hi, Kristen. How are you?" Foster spoke.

"I'm doing well." Then Kristen thanked him. "You are such kind and caring person. Thank you for everything. I loved those beautiful flowers you sent today. I don't know how I can ever repay you."

Foster replied, "You don't have to Kristen. You're my friend."

"Absolutely, Foster," Kristen assured. "Sorry I called you in middle of the day."

"No worries," Foster told Kristen. "Please call me anytime."

"Ah, that's so sweet of you." Kristen smiled. "Thank you, Foster. I will let you go."

Foster's secretary, Ms. Kerry, couldn't stop herself from saying, "I have never seen you so happy in such a long time."

Foster smiled and said, "Thank you."

* * * * *

It wouldn't be long until Kristen found out, surprisingly, that Margaret was being discharged from the facility.

"My dear, never forget who you are," Margaret announced.

Kristen, overwhelmed by the news of Margaret's departure, couldn't hold back the tears. She cried. "I hope that we can continue this relationship?" Kristen sobbed.

"Oh, my dear, you know you will always have a special place in my heart," Margaret announced. "I have a feeling this will not be the last time we will see each other."

Through the tears, Kristen leaned over in her wheelchair and graciously held Margaret until she felt her grip just could not hold on any longer.

"I will miss you so much," Kristen said. "You have been my saving grace during this trial."

Margaret glanced at Kristen in confidence and picked up her bags. Then she kissed Kristen on the forehead.

Kristen was unsure what the future held after Margaret left. Would Foster still come around even after his aunt was discharged? Hopefully. As for Kristen, she understood that nothing was certain. She soon found out that Michael had been cheating on her with his intern. Everything that had accumulated over the months was just short to nothing, giving Kristen a false sense of hope that she'd ever find a man who will be faithful.

The good news though is that Foster kept coming to see her. He did not abandon Kristen or give her a false sense of hope. The flowers kept coming, the conversations kept flowing, and the random phone calls kept ringing. Kristen drowned out the thought of Michael's unfaithfulness and instead focused totally on Foster's love. That's really all that mattered for her well-being.

Kristen improved greatly with physical therapy and moved from a wheelchair to crutches. She was well on her way to recovery. Doctors said it will likely take twelve weeks for Kirsten to fully heal and get back to normal weight-bearing activities. Foster applauded Kristen's improvements. He became Kristen's corner cheerleader, except without the pom-poms and silly skirt. He was a verbal juggernaut for Kristen's positive support team.

* * * * *

Kristen's discharge paperwork came forward. She was being released from the skilled nursing facility and granted the opportunity to go home. It only took Kristen a few weeks to recover and reach her goals. Foster took the initiative to pick Kristen up and give her a ride home. He picked her up in his BMW 5 Series, which, for Kristen, was a little over the top. Foster, though, never boasted about his luxury. Instead, he was very humble in spirit.

"You know, Foster, I was really depressed until I met you," Kristen announced. "Thank you for taking the time from your busy schedule to be with me."

"You have no idea how much you mean to me," Foster responded. "You are a wonderful person."

"Well, I appreciate you," Kristen stated.

"Sometimes bad things happen to good people," Foster said. "But if bad things didn't happen, I would have never met you."

Kristen smiled back with a gesture that agreed with Foster's statement. Kristen looked off in the distance as she took in all the beauty of Chicago's landscape. Kristen had no idea how much she enjoyed the city until she was kept cooped up in the nursing facility for so many weeks. However, Kristen did appreciate all the care she received. And it was hard to even say goodbye to all the nursing staff.

Foster dropped Kristen off at her apartment. He ran around to Kristen's passenger side door, unclipped the seat belt, and grabbed her crutches. Foster should have been a caretaker as evidenced by his natural ability to care for Kristen. But Kristen was never a codependent individual; she was an independent woman looking for true love.

"Call me once you get settled," Foster said.

"I most certainly will," Kristen responded.

Cathy met Kristen and Foster at the door. Cathy bypassed Foster and gripped Kristen, almost taking the breath out of her lungs. Kristen then introduced Foster to Cathy.

"I've heard a lot about you," Cathy stated.

"Hopefully all good things." Foster chuckled.

"That's for me to know and you to find out." Cathy smiled back.

Foster kissed Kristen on the forehead and allowed Cathy to take ownership of Kristen's things.

* * * * *

One week had gone by, and instead of Kristen calling Foster, he surprisingly called her.

"How are you feeling?" Foster asked.

"I'm doing well. Thanks for asking," Kristen responded.

"Any big plans for today?" Foster continued.

"Not much. Cathy is going to dinner with her boyfriend," Kristen said.

"In that case, would you mind going to dinner with me?" Foster asked.

"I'm still on crutches," Kristen stated.

"Don't worry about that," Foster assured. "I'll pick you up at six p.m."

* * * *

Foster picked Kristen up in his luxurious BMW again. It was a little tight for Kristen's disability. But Foster was a MacGyver for eloquently placing Kristen in the seat. Foster closed the door and placed Kristen's crutches in the back seat.

"Where would you like to eat?" Foster asked.

"Anything would be fine," Kristen responded.

"I know a great Italian restaurant that would be perfect," Foster exclaimed.

"Sure," Kristen responded.

The two showed up at the restaurant on Lakeshore Drive, just near Lake Michigan. The moon was full. Kristen could see the glare of the moon shining off the lake's surface. The ambiance was perfect. There were clean tabletops with flawless silverware, and Kristen could see her reflection in them. She may have checked her hair with the spoon she picked up. Foster laughed at Kristen's self-appreciation when he caught her in the act.

"This is so romantic, Foster," Kristen stated.

"I knew you would like it," Foster responded.

Foster was overtaken by the beauty in Kristen: her blond hair and blue eyes, her stunning dress that would catch the eye of the paparazzi had Kristen been a celebrity. In Foster's eyes, she was a celebrity.

"Look at the reflection of the moon off the water," Foster said.

"Oh yes, so beautiful!" Kristen stated.

"Much like you," Foster spoke softly.

"I feel so good when I'm with you," Kristen said. "Nothing bothers me." Kristen reached over and gently took Foster's hand.

Moments like these were what Kristen envisioned as a young girl, dreaming of finding Mr. McDreamy one day. Foster seemed like the perfect package: tall, handsome, well-dressed with a gentle heart to care for others, and no strings attached—just love.

Kristen noticed the expensive meals that were on the menu. Foster noticed them too but was not put off by the prices.

"You make me forget every pain that I have," Kristen stated.

"Me too," Foster announced. "You help give me a break from my hectic week."

The dinner was over the top. Kristen felt adored. The meal was flawless. It was a five-course meal, and Kristen devoured every delicacy that came her way. She saw Foster slowly taking in every bite as well. But Kristen had to slow her pace and not stuff her face.

After dinner, Foster took her home. He helped get her out of the car and chaperoned her to the front door. He hugged her, and Kristen leaned in for a good-night kiss.

"Thank you so much for a wonderful dinner," Kristen said.

"Don't mention it," Foster responded. "It was my pleasure."

*　*　*　*

Later the next day, Kristen notices that Cathy is not herself. She wonders if anything has happened to Cathy. Cathy tells Kristen nothing is wrong.

"Shall we go out for dinner?" Kristen asked Cathy.

"Sounds great, Kristen," Cathy agreed.

Kristen knew something was going on with Cathy but didn't want to bother her. Instead, she wanted Cathy to just tell her.

"Where do you want to eat?" Kristen asked.

Cathy suggested a regular pizza place.

"Okay, Cathy," Kristen said. "Let's go."

They ordered their favorite pepperoni pizza. While waiting for the order, they talked about their early days in Chicago.

"I know, Kristen," Cathy fondly remembered.

"Never thought I would be moving to Chicago for a job," Kristen said. "But I have no regrets though."

Cathy was still not in mood to talk. Usually, she was bubbly and a nonstop talker. Kristen told Cathy she knows there's something she's hiding.

Cathy opened up.

"I had a big fight with Craig last night," Cathy said. She confided to Kristen of an argument she had with her boyfriend. "He said he will never talk to me again." Cathy explained what led to the fight. "He promised me that he wouldn't drink alcohol anymore, but he lied. And I think he has an addiction problem. He said he was trying hard to quit. In fact, he did quit drinking alcohol for six months, before he started again. He also has his friends who do drugs, and they are binge drinkers too."

"I know what you are saying, Cathy," Kristen suggested. "But you know he loves you madly."

"Well, that's true," Cathy stated. "But I don't want him to drink so much that he damages his liver for good."

Kristen and Cathy received the pizza they ordered.

Cathy took one slice and started eating. It was so hot, she burned her tongue. She gulps a big drink of her Coke to relieve that burning sensation. It appeared she was very hungry. Kristen laughed as she watched Cathy's reaction.

"You know, Cathy, Craig will probably call you by tomorrow," Kristen stated.

"I don't think so," Cathy disagreed. "He was mad. This time he was serious."

"But I strongly believe he will," Kristen insisted.

"Wow, the pizza tastes good, Kristen," Cathy said excitedly.

"Yep, you are right, Cathy," Kristen agreed.

"How about you take that last slice," Kristen suggested to Cathy.

"I'm full," Cathy said.

"Okay then," Kristen said.

They received their bill for the pizza, and Kristen offered to pay for it.

"Thank you, Kristen," Cathy said.

"You are welcome, Cathy," Kristen stated.

* * * * *

The following day Cathy received a beautiful bouquet of roses with a card.

The card said, "Thinking of you. Love you, my sweetheart, Craig."

Kristen admired the flowers. "Oh my, such beautiful roses," Kristen said excitedly. "Who sent them, Cathy?"

Cathy couldn't hold back her emotions and told Kristen it was Craig who sent them.

"I told you, Cathy," Kristen reminded.

"Yes, you are right, Kristen," Cathy admitted.

Cathy hugged Kristen. "You are my big sister," Cathy told Kristen.

"Well, you are going to meet him, right?" Kristen said.

"I think so," Cathy promised.

Kristen smiled. "Any way, I'm going to be late getting back to the office," Kristen said. "We will catch up this evening."

"Sure, Kristen," Cathy replied.

* * * * *

The months went by, and Kristen and Foster grew closer and closer. Much like a perfectly garnished side to a course, Kristen felt the tug of her heart grow larger for Foster. He, in return, felt the adherence to Kristen's life and knew that they had been intended to meet.

Kristen happened to be on the phone with Foster while he was at lunch with a group for a meeting. Kristen couldn't ignore the sudden abdominal pain and felt like she was about to pass out.

She told Foster while he was on the phone, "I'm not feeling well."

"What's wrong?" Foster responded.

"I don't know," Kristen said. "I feel like I'm going to pass out."

"Do you need me to call an ambulance?" Foster rushed.

"No, I'll call," Kristen responded.

"Okay, I'm on my way," Foster said. "I'm right near you."

Foster jumped into his BMW and hightailed it down the street. Foster was driving fast to reach Kristen's apartment and, in the process, caught the attention of a police officer. It happened to be John. So John put on the flashing lights and stopped Foster. He walked slowly to driver's side and said to Foster, "Sir, you were going fifteen miles over the speed limit."

"I was in hurry to reach my friend who is having life-threatening GI bleeding," Foster pleaded.

Believing Foster, John asked him to follow his police car. Foster thanked God. He reached Kristen's apartment in no time at all with help of John.

Foster met the ambulance that was sitting in front of Kristen's apartment with flashing lights. He rushed up the stairs and peeked in the opened apartment door. The paramedics had already started the IVs, and they were taking vital signs. Kristen appeared pale and weak. Foster crouched down and held Kristen's hand for support.

"Looks like she has lost a significant amount of blood," the paramedic stated. "We need to move quickly."

Kristen did let the paramedics know that she had been losing a lot of blood through her rectum for the past couple days. And she had begun vomiting blood just today. She also reported that she'd been taking an excess amount of ibuprofen to help with her pain instead of opioids.

Kristen's blood pressure was low. The paramedics quickly infused a bag of normal saline to help bring her pressure up. Kristen used all the strength she could to try and appease Foster by smiling at him.

Foster had tears in his eyes while attempting to control his emotions. He was quickly on the phone with one of his buddies, an associate professor with the gastroenterology department.

"Hello, Silverstein?" Foster stated. "I need your help taking care of my friend, Kristen."

"Sure, Foster," Dr. Silverstein responded. "I'm here on call now."

"Great, she is coming by ambulance to Northwestern," Foster said.

"Okay, see you in a few minutes," Dr. Silverstein closed.

The paramedics hoisted Kristen on the stretcher and placed her in the ambulance.

John was waiting outside the apartment. He recognized Kristen right away.

"Hello, Kristen," John spoke. "Well, I can explain later, Kristen."

"Please take care of her," Foster pleaded. "She is an angel in human form."

"Sure," John assured. "She helped me find my daughter by publishing poems I had written in the *Chicago Tribune*."

"Thank you for believing me and not giving me a speeding ticket," Foster said.

"Thank you, John."

"Anytime, my child," John replied. John told Kristen that he would see her at the hospital.

The sirens were deafening in the streets. Foster jumped in his vehicle behind the ambulance. Kristen was scared, as bags of IV solution hung above her stretcher. She knew Foster was near, which for her brought much more comfort than the paramedics.

The ambulance reached Northwestern Hospital and pushed Kristen through the bay doors. She was met by health-care professionals. They had already received reports over the intercom. Dr. Silverstein, the gastroenterologist, met Kristen just like Foster had asked. He let Kristen know that she'd likely developed a gastric ulcer from the amount of ibuprofen she ingested for pain. They were cross-matching her for three units to stabilize the bleed.

It was for certain that things were moving quickly. Nevertheless, Foster was at her bedside every minute, helping to make sure she was safe and not alone. As for the both of them though, they had no idea what the outcome of this situation would entail. They both just knew they had each other.

Chapter

8

The health-care workers had to move fast to prep Kristen for an upper endoscopy to find the bleed. Dr. Silverstein was considered one of the greatest gastrointestinal physicians at Northwestern, likely in the state. So Foster knew she was in good hands.

* * * * *

The procedure was completed, and Kristen awoke slowly from the anesthesia. She softly opened her eyes and saw Foster right in front of her. Her blurred, vacant vision was beginning to clear and she saw Foster's gleaming smile.

"Hello, Kristen," Foster announced.

Kristen couldn't help but feel butterflies in her stomach, or maybe it was the postprocedural nausea she was feeling.

"How are you feeling?" Foster asked.

"I'm feeling fine," Kristen responded. "Thank you for being here."

Foster leaned in and gripped Kristen's hand from under the covers. The touch of Foster's hand was comforting, as if Kristen felt every emotion he was hiding deep inside his soul.

Dr. Silverstein entered the room.

"Hello, Kristen," Dr. Silverstein said. "How are you feeling?"

"Fine, Doctor," Kristen responded.

"Everything went well," Dr. Silverstein announced. "Couldn't have gone better."

Dr. Silverstein then explained the reason for her bleed. She had a duodenal ulcer that was bleeding uncontrollably. Luckily for Kristen, he was able to place five clips within her intestine and an epinephrine injection to constrict her vessels.

"I believe the bleed occurred from the amount of ibuprofen," Dr. Silverstein stated. "You need to avoid them from here on out." Instead, Dr. Silverstein recommended that she take Prilosec for her continuing treatment of the ulcer.

They moved Kristen to an ICU room for close monitoring. Her blood work came back flawless, and her hemoglobin and hematocrit were stable as well. Everything seemed to be going well.

Foster was like a leech, suctioned to Kristen's every move. He did not let her out of his sight, not even for a minute.

"I called Cathy," Foster said. "I convinced her to stay home and that you were stable."

"Thank you so much for doing that," Kristen responded.

Foster had pulled up a recliner in Kristen's room as the nurses were giving her more pain medication. Kristen soon drifted off, and Foster kept watch throughout the night until he too fell sound asleep.

The nurses had to write down Kristen's routine vitals and check on her breathing. As they were panning over Kristen's wires and checking her pulse, the alarms started to sound. Suddenly, the staff was pushing Foster out the door and having him wait outside. They pressed the code-blue button.

Foster saw the rush of nurses and doctors swoop into Kristen's room and surround her with machines. An overhead voice repeated, "Code blue," over the speakers throughout the hospital. Foster could feel his heart racing and his breathing move at a rapid rate.

Out of nowhere, miraculously, the staff got a pulse. Kristen started to have shallow breaths. Everyone in the room was relieved. Foster felt weak.

The staff approached Foster and told him that everything is going to be fine.

"Foster," Kristen softly spoke. "Foster, are you awake?"

Foster suddenly jumped up out of his recliner, drenched in sweat and breathing fast.

"Are you okay?" Kristen asked. "You don't look so good."

"I must've had a bad dream," Foster replied.

Foster got up slowly to drift toward Kristen's hospital bed. He held on to her hand gently again.

"I can't believe you were with me all night," Kristen announced.

"It's not a problem," Foster replied.

"I am so lucky to have you in my life," Kristen said.

"You don't have to worry about a thing," Foster replied. "I'm here to stay. How's your pain?"

"Much better," Kristen spoke.

In midconversation, Cathy entered the room.

"Oh my gosh, Kristen," Cathy said. "What happened to you?"

"Well, let's just say I was well taken care of," Kristen said as she smiled at Foster. Kristen insisted that Foster take a break and head home to freshen up. Foster kissed Kristen on the forehead and exited the room.

Dr. Silverstein entered the room next.

"How are you feeling, Kristen?" Dr. Silverstein asked.

"Much better," Kristen replied.

"Everything is looking good," Dr. Silverstein said. "If your numbers continue to look good, I will discharge you in a day or two."

"Thank you so much for all your help," Kristen stated.

"It's my pleasure," Dr. Silverstein responded. "Looks like luck was on your side."

* * * * *

They soon transferred Kristen to the medical unit as a step down from the ICU. Kristen was thrilled that everything seemed to be working out, and she anticipated being discharged in a couple days. It was a relief to know she had two things going well for her: a man with a compassionate heart and a doctor with compassionate hands.

John visited Kristen the day after her endoscopy.

"How are you doing, Kristen?" John asked.

"Doing well, John," Kristen responded. "They found the bleeder in my stomach and were able to stop it."

"Awesome!" John exclaimed. He brought flowers for Kristen.

"Thank you, John, for such beautiful flowers," Kristen said thoughtfully.

"You are welcome, Kristen," John stated. "Please call me if you need any help."

"Sure, John," Kristen promised. "My mom will be here soon."

"That's good," John replied.

John got a phone call.

"Kristen, I have to go, but I will call you tomorrow," John stated.

"Sure, John," Kristen said.

* * * * *

Finally, two days later, Kristen received the best news: she was going home. She was surrounded by an extravagant assortment of flowers that were displayed across her room, given by Foster. The staff even had a difficult time getting all the flowers into Kristen's vehicle. Foster thought it was funny to see an entire team attempt to place the flowers strategically in the back of his car. Nevertheless, Kristen could tangibly taste the love that was in the air.

After Foster had gotten Kristen home, he tucked her in tight and headed out the door to go back to his work.

* * * * *

It had been one year since her accident. She had forgotten a lot about what had happened in the aftermath of the tragedy. But out of the blue, she received a phone call. It was Michael.

"Hi, Kristen," Michael spoke softly. "How are you doing?"

Kristen could tell by the voice it was him. She felt a lot of the anger and bitterness brewing back inside her, and the words just came out.

"What do you want, Michael?" Kristen asked.

"Please, Kristen," Michael responded. "Give me a chance to explain."

"Why should I?" Kristen said.

"I agree, I don't deserve it," Michael responded. "Would you please meet me this coming Saturday?"

"No, Michael!" Kristen sternly said.

"I'm really sorry," Michael responded.

"You never even bothered to care," Kristen shouted. "Or cared to call me while I was in the hospital. You left me for someone else. And you called off our wedding at the last minute."

Michael tried to explain over the phone, but Kristen wasn't buying it, not for a minute. She hung up the phone quickly and took a long, deep sigh of relief.

"Who was that?" Cathy asked.

"It was Michael," Kristen replied. "Can you believe the nerve of that man?"

"How dare he even call you!" Cathy said, all worked up.

"Well, he pleaded that I meet with him this Saturday," Kristen said. "I told him no."

"Good, Kristen!" Cathy replied.

* * * * *

That night, Kristen had trouble sleeping. She thought about all her memories with Michael throughout the years—the highs and the lows, the romance and the heartbreak, every bit of it. Through her chaotic thoughts, Kristen finally decided to meet with Michael to hear what he had to say. Not that it would change anything, but maybe, in some sense, she wanted closure. So Kristen dressed up for dinner and headed to the restaurant. In the back of her mind, Kristen wondered if she was even doing the right thing.

Michael greeted Kristen at the restaurant. He was floating. Seeing Kristen rekindled much of what he knew he'd lost. Kristen, however, was closed off. Her thoughts were not positive toward Michael. She was basically there to appease Michael's request. They both sat down calmly without any fireworks to start off the night.

"How are you doing?" Michael asked.

"Fine," Kristen replied.

"You look beautiful," Michael announced.

They kept their distance. No hugging, and absolutely no kissing. Like two opposite worlds with no gravitational pull toward one another, they simply kept the peace.

"I'll be brutally honest with you," Michael said. "My marriage didn't last six months because she doesn't love me anymore."

"Sorry to hear that, Michael," Kristen said. "I know what that's like."

"I deserved it," Michael said. "I caused you so much pain and embarrassment by my actions."

Michael went into full details about how they planned to live their lives together. He explained to Kristen that it was the best time of his life and that he realized what he'd lost and how foolish he was as well but there is nothing he can do to change that now.

Real tears started to stream down the sides of his face. Kristen could tell he was sincere. But it didn't matter. Kristen's built-up bitterness toward Michael started to surface.

"You know, Michael," Kristen spoke. "You left me in the middle of the road. You didn't care how I recovered after the wreck. I cried for months after you left me. I felt like committing suicide at times. But I drew strength from my Lord, Jesus Christ. I am now a better person."

Kristen didn't have one tear to drop. It was likely that the strength she built from the wreck and the acute bleed helped build her character into who she is now: a Wonder Woman! Kristen had confidence in what she wanted and who she wanted to spend the rest of her life with now.

Kristen unloaded on Michael like a machine gun. Word after word shredded Michael's flesh, and he could feel the break in his skin open old wounds. Michael, in return, practically begged Kristen to take him back.

"I wish you the best, Michael," Kristen stated kindly.

The two finished their meals and got up from the table. Michael was kicking himself knowing that he'd lost Kristen for good. Clearly,

Michael was disappointed, and it was easy to tell by the look in his eyes. It would be the last time Michael would lay eyes on Kristen as they cordially exited the restaurant together.

Kristen turned to Michael and gave him one more good smile and then said goodbye. The night was a disaster for Michael, but for Kristen it felt like victory. She kept her composure and didn't shed one tear. But something inside Kristen's genuine heart made her wonder if she was too hard on Michael. But it was nothing compared to what she went through when they were engaged. And this convinced her that she had done the right thing.

Besides, Kristen had her eyes set on someone else. And his name is Foster. And he is everything she had hoped for in a man.

She made her way back home to meet with Cathy for the evening.

"How did your evening go?" Cathy asked.

"I met with Michael," Kristen replied.

"And…?" Cathy responded.

"I wished him the best," Kristen said. "In some way, I wondered if I was too hard on him. But then I thought about all the heartache moments with him and convinced myself that life is going to be all right."

"I'm so proud of you, Kristen," Cathy said.

"I'm actually kind of proud of myself too," Kristen replied.

Chapter

9

Because of some unforeseen circumstance, Kristen left her position at the health insurance company and moved to another position. Because of her time away from work, Kristen felt the tug of being pulled in a different direction. Kristen's accident had given her time and space to think. Kristen thought about the new life she wanted to have. And she had an entirely new perspective on life: that it is short, and there are meaningful things to explore in this world.

Foster encouraged Kristen to apply at his workplace. Little did Kristen know that Foster was the CEO of his own company.

"It will be a fresh start for you and more opportunities to grow," said Foster as he nudged her side, encouraging Kristen to take the leap. "Here's a contact number to our human resources."

Foster was never the bragging type. He had everything in the palm of his hands as far as success and status. But with Kristen, he never boasted about his abilities. This is likely why Kristen found him to be even more charming, aside from his good looks.

The next day, Kristen called HR and sent over her CV by fax to see if she was even qualified for the position.

Foster told Kristen, "Don't worry about it. It's done."

Because of the confidence as to how that statement sounded, Kristen thought maybe he was in good standing with the administrator there. Oh, how oblivious she was to her surroundings, not that the fragrance of Foster's presence had anything to do with it.

Kristen made her entry into the lobby, where there was a plethora of other applicants.

If it is supposed to be, Kristen thought, *all things will work out and I'll get the position.* Kristen fully trusted her experience.

They called her to the back room where interviews were taking place.

"Please have a seat," the interviewer stated. "There is a lot I want to hear about why we need to hire you."

They went into details about Kristen's software experience. Kristen might as well have just said she was from Microsoft based on the depth of her knowledge. Kristen answered all the questions thoroughly and accurately. She was in for sure.

"You're hired," the interviewer quickly announced.

"Well, that was easy," Kristen bashfully responded.

"Let's just say a little bug told me about you beforehand," the interviewer responded.

Kristen confidently strutted out the room into the lobby. Everyone noticed by the confident steps in Kristen's walk that she had landed the job. It was almost as if all the other candidates wanted to just get up and walk out the door in defeat. Kristen was on cloud nine for sure.

* * * *

Foster had taken Kristen out on a routine elegant dinner to celebrate her victory in landing the job at his workplace. They were both buzzing to the same tune. Kristen thanked Foster for helping her land the position. And Foster was humbled that he'd been able to help.

"Excuse me," said Kristen as she got up to go to the restroom.

Being a gentleman, Foster stood up as Kristen left the table.

An old couple was sitting next to Foster's and Kristen's table.

"Oh, my she is so beautiful," the old lady complimented. "Is she your wife?"

"No, ma'am," Foster replied. "She is my girlfriend."

The old lady insisted, "You better propose to her before some-one else asks for her hand in marriage."

Foster smiled and said, "Thank you, ma'am."

While they were talking, Kristen returned from the bathroom. The old lady reminded Foster again about proposing to Kristen, while making eye contact with him.

Foster just smiled again.

"What's going on, Foster?" Kristen asked.

"Nothing," Foster replied. "We were just talking about how good the food is here."

"Yep, I agree, Foster," Kristen stated.

"You know, Kristen, you look beautiful in your lavender dress," Foster complimented.

"Thank you, Foster," Kristen replied. "I always feel so happy when you are with me." But Kristen mumbled to herself, "I don't know how long this will last."

"What did you say, Kristen?" Foster asked.

"Nothing, Foster," Kristen deflected. "I was just thinking that you are going to be pulled away from me soon by some beautiful woman."

"Really?" Foster laughed.

"You are so kind, handsome, and well-accomplished," Kristen insisted. "Any woman would say yes to you, Foster."

"Oh, come on, Kristen," Foster exclaimed.

"I truly believe it, Foster," Kristen insisted.

"What can I say, Kristen," Foster kidded.

And they both laughed together.

They continued their conversation over dinner, and Foster picked up the check as they strolled out the door into the alley.

Suddenly, someone from the dark alley jumped out and demanded money from them. Foster attempted to calm the person down while leaping in front of Kristen. In the process, the man slashed Foster's hand. It happened so fast; it was difficult for Foster to grasp what had happened.

Fortunately, there happened to be witnesses that came into the spotlight and caused the suspected robber to flee off into the night.

Kristen was in shock as she noticed the blood dripping from Foster's hand.

"We need to get you to the hospital," Kristen shrieked.

"It doesn't hurt," Foster responded. "I'll be okay."

Kristen demanded that Foster go to the hospital. She wrapped his hand with her scarf and squeezed the tourniquet tight.

"Give me the keys, Foster," Kristen demanded.

"No, I can drive," Foster responded.

"I insist," Kristen stated. "Let me drive."

Foster had no other option. As he noticed the look in Kristen's eyes, there was simply no way for him to rebut her forceful approach to help. So he tossed the keys across the hood and gently and willingly got into the passenger side of the vehicle.

As Kristen was driving, she kept pressure on his hand, even though he didn't need any more help. Kristen pulled into the parking lot of urgent care and rushed Foster inside to check in. They were both greeted in the room by the physician after the nurse had walked them both back. Foster explained to the physician that he didn't get a good look at the man's face but knew he had a knife. He protected Kristen. Foster was willing to even take a bullet for her if need be.

"We need to clean the wound," the physician stated. "And suture you up."

Foster agreed to the service. They cleansed his wound and gave him a tetanus shot. They applied Betadine for sterility and placed multiple sutures to his dorsal hand.

"I will need you to come back in one week for suture removal," stated the physician. "And a little pain medication to get you by."

"There's no need for a doctor," Foster replied. "I will be fine."

At this point in time, Kristen was unsure if her adrenaline was wearing off due to the shock, but she began to cry. She held Foster's hand tightly and questioned all the moments leading up to the event.

"It could have happened anywhere, Kristen," Foster reassured her.

"It makes me feel bad," Kristen responded.

After Foster was discharged, they went home, with Kristen driving him home.

"I've never seen your place," Kristen stated.

"You can stay with me tonight, if you want?" Foster suggested.

"I'll stay and make sure you are all right," Kristen responded.

Foster had pointed Kristen to their destination. He had his own parking space, which for Kristen, seemed a little over the top. She handed Foster the keys, and they both held hand while walking into the apartment complex. They got in the elevator and pressed floor 20. Kristen started to ponder how well her new job might pay based on where Foster lived. Money must have been good with this company.

Foster unlocked the door after walking down the hallway to the only apartment on the twentieth floor.

"Wow, what a nice apartment," Kristen outspokenly said.

"Would you like something to drink?" Foster asked.

"Sure," Kristen responded.

At this point, Kristen felt out of her element. The windows cascaded across the apartment and you could see the city as if you were viewing it through a big-screen television. The lighting, the furniture, and the kitchen were all immaculate. It almost seemed as if Kristen was lounging with the president himself.

Kristen jokingly asked, "Do you cook, Foster?"

"Why, yes," Foster responded.

Observing Foster's apartment in the shape it is in, Kristen could have sworn he had his own chef. Maybe he did? Also a housekeeper. It wouldn't be surprising if he had his own valet as well. Kristen chuckled a bit under her breath as she thought about all these questions. Foster observed that Kristen was summoning something up because her face revealed as such.

The two had great conversations well into the evening about Kristen's childhood. At one point, Foster snuck out to smoke a cigarette, but Kristen didn't care for that at all.

Kristen dozed off on the couch. She was mumbling to Foster, "I love you. Don't ever leave me."

Foster couldn't help but smile knowing that the truth was coming out during Kristen's slumber.

He picked her up and carried her to his bedroom. He softly pulled back his sheets and tucked her in gently. He walked back into the living room and slept on the sofa.

* * * *

The next morning, after Kristen awoke in Foster's bed, she had forgotten about falling asleep on the couch. But there was no Foster.

Kristen walked out of the bedroom and caught Foster sleeping softly on the sofa. Impressed that he didn't take advantage of her during the night made Kristen adores him that much more. She walked over and kissed him on the forehead. Foster stretched his arms out as he felt the touch of her lips.

"Good morning," Foster announced.

"Well, good morning, sleepyhead," Kristen replied. "You slept here last night?"

"Yes," Foster responded. "I didn't want to bother you."

"Well, aren't you just the sweetest." Kristen blushed.

"How about breakfast?" Foster asked.

"Oh, you think you're that good, huh?" Kristen smiled.

"Better than deserved," Foster responded.

Foster brewed some fresh coffee and served them a well-prepared breakfast. Kristen was fulfilled both emotionally and physically. Kristen asked what happened last night. Foster told her that she dozed off on the couch. He felt sorry for her, so he carried her to his room.

"So you picked me up with your injured hand?" Kristen interrupted.

"Well, yes. But no worries," Foster responded. "My hand is already much better."

This night, though, was filled with chaos and compassion; and it took their relationship to new levels. Kristen nursed Foster's hand, and Foster showed Kristen his place. The two meshed well together. Like fine wine, their love fermented into a beautiful product. Kristen could feel the passion between them. It was something she felt with

Michael, except Foster was different—a lot different. He waited on her hand and foot and didn't care about what others thought.

In the same sense, Foster was growing deeper in love with Kristen, as both her beauty and care for him developed into a tangible piece of art, something not purchased with human hands. This is what true love is all about: giving up each other's interests for the sake of another and being knit together through experiences and seeing more of each other's character every day.

Foster didn't want to dare yet reveal that he was a successful CEO of his company, the one Kristen now worked for. He wanted Kristen to see him and only him—not his money, status, or capital.

Chapter

10

Foster had just walked into his office on the third floor of his company. Dressed to the gills with an Armani suit, he struck everyone's attention. Everyone stopped what they were doing to take a fine look at a man who was their boss.

Foster leaned over one of the accountants and asked her where Kristen's desk would be. The woman was breathless to even see Foster's lips moving so close to her. She mumbled as though speaking a different language and just pointed in the cubby next to her. She voiced to him that she'd be back any minute.

Kristen had made her way around the corner. In her arms was an abundance of files she collected from around the company. Foster quickly stood up as Kristen approached her own desk. Kristen was stunned to see Foster so dressed up. He looked like a movie actor in the pristine suit he was wearing, almost as if he just walked off the red carpet.

"Well, I thought I would drop by and see if you wanted to join me for lunch?" Foster said.

"How about walking me to the coffee place?" Kristen responded. "I have a lot to do and learn here."

The two walked in sync with one another. And all the employees in the background were whispering, "She is so lucky."

"Well, how is your new job?" Foster asked.

"It's really nice," Kristen responded. "A great change."

"I'm glad everything is going well," Foster stated.

"You are like a lucky charm for me," Kristen replied. "I never want to lose you."

"You won't," Foster replied.

As the two were chatting over coffee, Kristen's boss showed up. Kristen attempted to get up, but he gestured her to stay seated. Foster gave him a firm handshake and winked at him. You see, Kristen still had no idea Foster was running the show. He'd told everyone, under the radar, to not make any mention that he is the CEO of the company.

"Nice to meet you, Foster," Kristen's boss stated.

"Pleasure is mine," Foster replied.

After Kristen's boss left, Foster complimented him on how great a boss he was to her. Foster also mentioned that Kristen was very lucky to have people like him at her job. Kristen agreed. The two parted ways as Foster had meetings to attend and Kristen had a lot of training to complete. The two kissed and headed their separate ways.

* * * * *

Later that night, Cathy gets a frantic call at 11:00 p.m. that Craig was arrested by police and will be taken to jail. Cathy was crying loudly.

Kristen ran into Cathy's room.

"What happened, Cathy?" Kristen asked anxiously.

"Oh my gosh!" Cathy said. "Craig was arrested."

There was a fight that had broken out between two gangs. And Craig was with one of the gangs.

"My boyfriend said he will be taken to court tomorrow," Cathy said frantically. "He was really scared, and I could tell that by his trembling voice. I don't know what to do Kristen."

Kristen tells Cathy not to worry and that they'd figure out how to help.

"Let me call John," Kristen suggested.

Cathy mentioned that since it's 11:00 p.m., maybe John had gone to sleep.

"It's okay, let me call him," Kristen said.

So Kristen calls John on his cell phone.

"Sorry to call you this late, John," Kristen apologized.

"No worries, Kristen," John assured.

So Kristen tells John that her roommate Cathy's boyfriend had been arrested at a downtown restaurant.

"There was a shootout between two gangs," Kristen explained to John. "Cathy's boyfriend was with one of those gangs. Apparently, he was at the wrong place and wrong time."

"Yeah, I heard about it," John stated.

"We are about to go see him," Kristen informed John.

"Don't worry, I will be there by the time you get there," John said.

"Thank you, John," Kristen stated. "I really appreciate it."

"I know a good friend of mine who is an attorney, and he can take care of it," John stated. "I have known him for a long time. He is an excellent attorney. I will call him now."

"Thank you, John," Kristen said, relieved.

"You are welcome, Kristen," John replied.

* * * * *

Cathy and Kristen got into the car and drove to the police station. John was already there with his friend Robert, the attorney.

"Hello, Kristen and Cathy," John spoke.

Cathy was crying. John consoled Cathy, and Robert told Cathy not to worry. John paid the bond money for Craig. Robert filled out the paperwork and took care of the bail for Craig.

Kristen hugged John and said, "Thank you. I appreciate it."

John's colleague, who passed by, asked him if Kristen is his daughter.

"You can say that," John suggested.

Kristen smiled, accepting John's response.

* * * * *

Cathy hugged Craig, who was obviously shaken up. Craig promised that he will never mingle with any gang members again. Cathy and

Craig tell John how appreciative and thankful they are for him being there for them.

John reminded Cathy that he is glad to help her because she is Kristen's best friend.

"What I can say," John stated. "It's my pleasure. Any time."

"Well, it's getting late for you all," Robert reminded them. "We will go to court tomorrow to represent Craig."

John told Craig that he needs to explain everything to Robert that took place at the restaurant.

"Sure, I will John," Craig promised.

John got a call on his mobile unit about a robbery at a local gas station.

"Okay, guys, I need to go," John said.

Kristen told John to be careful. John promised Kristen that he will be careful.

Cathy told Kristen how lucky she is having her in her life.

"Cathy, you would have done the same for me if you were in my place," Kristen assured.

Craig was feeling guilty about putting everyone into trouble. Craig looked at Kristen and said, "Thank you. It means a lot to me all that you have done tonight."

"You are welcome, Craig," Kristen replied.

They headed out. Kristen and Cathy dropped Craig off at his apartment before going to their place.

"Craig, please do follow up with Robert in the morning," Cathy asked. "Don't screw it up."

"I will follow up with Robert, and I won't screw it up, Cathy," Craig promised.

*　*　*　*

Kristen was feeling sleepy. Cathy noticed that Kristen is sleepy and asked if she wanted her to drive.

"No, Cathy, we are almost there," Kristen responded.

Since they were both so tired, they went to bed right away. They obviously had to get up early since the following day was a workday.

* * * * *

Kristen was at work when she received a call from Cathy that Craig was cleared of any charges and was only warned not to be involved with any more gang activities.

"Wow, that's great news, Cathy!" Kristen stated.

"Please tell John that how grateful we are for his help," Cathy said.

"Sure, I will, Cathy," Kristen promised.

Kristen called John.

"Hello, Kristen," John said.

"John, Craig was cleared from any wrongdoing," Kristen told him.

"Yep, Robert just informed me of that," John replied.

"Thank you, John," a grateful Kristen said. "I really appreciate it."

"Anytime, my child," John said.

"Ah, you are so kind," Kristen responded. "We'll keep in touch."

"Sure, Kristen," John replied.

* * * * *

Kristen was invited to a St. Patrick's Day party in downtown Chicago. Foster introduced her to a couple of his colleagues. They had girlfriends with them.

"So how long have you known Foster," the girls asked.

"About one year," Kristen replied.

"How did you meet?" they continued.

"It's a long story," Kristen responded.

They continued their conversation over beer, green beer that is. They chuckled over small jokes and a decent amount of liquor. There was loud music in the background, and Kristen took in the river that was turned green every St. Patrick's Day.

"You know, Foster is a great guy," the women stated.

"Yes, I know," Kristen replied.

"He gives his life to something if he likes someone," the women continued.

Into the night, Kristen kept getting compliments.

"You look beautiful."

"Very pretty."

"Gorgeous dress."

Kristen was in her element. While having her man by her side and great friends, much of what Kristen had been experiencing is a life that was to come.

"Would you like to come to Vegas with us next weekend?" the women asked. "They are having a business meeting and we have all been invited. Us girls can hang out."

Las Vegas sounded thrilling to Kristen. Chicago was as far as she had gone growing up. She was used to the small town of Potomac. Vegas was something she heard about growing up, but it was for more of the "fast lane" civilians, not Kristen.

"Oh, come on," the women insisted. "It will be fun!"

They urged Foster to invite her.

"If you don't have plans," Foster stated. "I would love for you to join us."

"Yes, I'll come!" Kristen responded.

"I will take reservations for our flight and hotel," Foster responded.

The words from Kristen's mouth came out faster than her brain could think. Just knowing Foster was going and being spontaneous about it is something that nudged her to agree. Kristen was getting out of her comfort zone. And for the life of her, that's all she worked with at this point. It had been all about being comfortable and never taking any risks—that is, until she met Foster.

Kristen said, "Excuse me" as she was going to the restroom.

As she was walking toward the restroom, Kristen caught the eyes of gang members who were there that night having fun. Three of them got up and slowly walked behind Kristen. The restroom was in the basement. John was also stationed in the same area because of a tip that some notorious gang members were going to be there. John saw Foster and Kristen going into the restaurant. He was an undercover cop that night. John wanted to see how Foster and Kristen were doing inside the restaurant. He knew the gang members were at this restaurant. He wanted to take a pee and went down to the men's restroom. The music was loud, and customers were having fun. The lights in the basement were little dim. The restroom was kept clean, and the lights were bright.

John was washing his hands when he heard loud voices in the hallway. Suddenly, the swinging door opened forcefully and in came three muscular-built men with tattoos on their faces forcing a lady into the men's restroom. One of them was holding a knife over her neck. You could see the fear and agony in her face. John realized right away that it was Kristen. He made eye contact with her in a way to let her know that everything will be okay. But Kristen was scared to death.

They shouted for everyone to get out now. Only one other person was there, and he ran out in time. John was walking calmly when one of the guys pushed him. John responded quickly, leaping on the guy who was holding the knife against Kristen's neck. John held him against the wall and told Kristen to go into one of restroom stalls and lock the door. John flipped one of those big guys on to the floor. And you could hear a big thud from his fall. The other two men tried to attack John. But being a combat veteran, it didn't take John much time to subdue the other two men. By now, the backup team had arrived. One of the guys hit John on the head with a beer bottle, which caused a cut over his forehead. Blood was dripping over his forehead. The three guys were arrested. Kristen walked out after hearing John say that everything is under control.

Kristen gasped. "Oh my god, what happened to your head?"

"It's just a superficial cut," John said.

Kristen hugged John and told him that he had saved her life.

"I don't know how I can thank you."

"You don't have to thank me."

Foster walked into scene. Kristen explained what had happened.

"John, you are a godsend in saving Kristen today," Foster kindly stated. "We really appreciate your help." Foster shook John's hands.

"You guys go ahead," John stated. "It's getting late."

"Sure, John," Foster agreed.

Kristen was shaken by the incident.

"I never thought these things could happen at a high-end restaurant." Kristen seemed puzzled. "I heard they are gang members and were drunk."

"Anyway, you are safe now," Foster comforted her. "John being there was a miracle."

Foster and Kristen both sent a thank-you card to John the following day.

Foster reminded Kristen about the Las Vegas trip that coming weekend.

"I know, Foster," Kristen replied. "I'm excited."

* * * * *

Foster picked up Kristen in his elegant car and arrived at the airport on time. He booked business-class tickets. Kristen had always walked past this section but had never been seated there. Of course, she was treated like royalty, being waited on hand and foot, and provided with all the luxury she had never received before. Honestly, she didn't know how to react, but she just went with it.

They arrived at their hotel by limousine. Foster booked the Bellagio, which is likely one of the best hotels on the strip. The group checked in, and butlers helped carry luggage to their room. Their suite was on the twelfth floor, facing the strip. Foster and Kristen waved the group to their room, and they headed to their own personal suite. The marble floors were mirroring their images. The door to their room was larger than some people's homes.

She made her way through the double doors and surveyed at the room as she walked into it. It was unreal. The suite was likely more than 1,200 square feet. Some vases were larger than her body. She felt like a princess in a fairy tale movie. Foster adored her childlike behavior. He took in every facial expression on Kristen's face.

Foster reminded Kristen that they had dinner reservations at 8:30 p.m. to meet back up with the group. He couldn't contain his excitement about surprising Kristen with the elegant dress he had purchased. He envisioned her radiant smile and the way her eyes would light up when she saw the cherry red dress adorned with brightly lit rhinestones. Foster left the dress hanging delicately on a hanger in the walk-in closet.

After Foster got ready, he met Kristen in the living room. Foster couldn't help but be captivated by Kristen's beauty as she stood before him in the cherry-red dress. "You look absolutely stunning."

Kristen blushed, a radiant smile gracing her lips. "Thank you, Foster. I can't believe you went through all this trouble. You've truly made tonight so special." She kissed him. Kristen's eyes met Foster's, and she saw the depth of his affection shining back at her. It was at that moment that the world around them seemed to fade away, leaving only their love-filled gaze. As they headed out into the night hand in hand, their steps light with anticipation, they savored each moment together.

Kristen enjoyed the water fountain, cascading in front of the Bellagio. The sounds of the slot machines excited her nerves. The amount of people dressed in tuxedos and nightwear was glamorous. Kristen was then handed $500 to go gamble a little bit. At first, she didn't want to take the money, but Foster insisted, and the women dragged her away for a little fun.

Kristen hit it big right out of the gate, while winning $10,000 on her third spin! She jumped up and down in her seat, not even knowing how much she won. She just saw the red light flicker above the machine and heard the loud siren coming from above.

Kristen handed Foster the money when they met back up, showing him how much she had won. The women were impressed by her actions. Now they all knew why Foster liked her so much.

After spending much time out on the strip and enjoying their elegant dinner, the women wanted to go back to the room to rest. Kristen was like a giddy schoolgirl, perplexed by the amount of energy she had with all the live action that happened in Las Vegas. Foster even chuckled at her childlike behavior. There was something about that nature that drew Foster's love for Kristen even deeper.

Once midnight struck, Foster and Kristen called it a night.

"We will see you guys in the morning," they shouted to the group.

As everyone made their way to the rooms, the front entrances softly drew shut, and the immaculate evening came to an end.

* * * * *

Foster had swiftly entered through their suite's front door with breakfast. Kristen, who was still asleep in their enormous, overcompensated bed, slowly arose with her hair half-kinked to the side. She smiled as she saw her prince charming walked across the room toward the bed.

"Breakfast in bed, I see," Kristen spoke.

"A breakfast fit for a queen," Foster replied.

The two continued conversation over breakfast, taking in all the excitement that happened the night prior. From all the sights and sounds to eloquent dress attire and everything in between, Kristen felt wooed by Foster's caretaking ability, while showing her his love through so much spontaneity.

After weighing in all on that happened, Foster and Kristen met back up with the group and checked out for the weekend. They had boarded back on their business-class airplane and flew back to Chicago. Las Vegas was like a dream but turning into a reality. Kristen began to understand how sheltered she was as a child. Not that her childhood was hindered by any means, but as an adult, Kristen got to witness life in full, living color.

* * * * *

Foster had pulled out two tickets to the Chicago Bulls basketball game that he purchased the week prior. Chicago Bulls red pumped through the streets of Chicago along with fandemonium any onlooker could see.

Kristen understood basketball living in Chicago, and this would be her opportunity to see what all the hype was about.

"Would you like to come with me?" Foster asked.

"Of course," Kristen replied, "I would love to see my first game!"

"You mean you have never been to a Chicago Bulls game before?" Foster responded.

"No," Kristen replied. "I always heard about them but never attended one before."

Foster was overtaken by the fact Kristen had never been to a Chicago Bulls game. He was uncertain if he should laugh or cry. Instead, he let out a soft chuckle. Kristen punched his arm, to make fun of her inadequacy as a Bulls fan. To Foster, living in Chicago and not attending a Bulls game was like entering an amusement park and never riding the rides.

Nevertheless, Foster met Kristen at the subway station at 6:00 p.m. They adventured their way toward the coliseum. The crowd grew larger as they got closer and closer to the door. It was like the Red Sea with all the red jerseys donned by all the fans.

Foster impressed Kristen even more with VIP seating. He obtained box seats through his company. Foster even had a custom-designed Bulls ball cap that he placed on her head when she got into the box. She pulled her thick blond hair through the back of the Starter cap to be initiated as a true fan of the Chicago Bulls franchise.

The scene Kristen witnessed through the glass was breathtaking. The loud music was sequenced with the players warming up, or so it seemed. You could hear the fans warming up by the waving arms she saw throughout the stadium. The lights panned across the people to highlight their facial expressions of joy and excitement.

Kristen took everything in, every sensual and emotional thought that was brought into her consciousness. Suddenly, she was met by other coworkers of Foster. These were the higher-ups who obviously had a persona about themselves and their work.

There were hors d'oeuvres appetizers and wine on stainless steel trays that were offered by the butlers. Kristen felt like sports met the queen's palace based on all she experienced here.

The game started, and Kristen met all of Foster's "accomplices." The rumble of the stadium was literally breathtaking. The announcer puffed up the fans and enticed them to get louder. She looked down at her wine glass, and it shook as if an earthquake was taking place. Kristen had no choice but to jump up and shout alongside them. Foster laughed as he saw that childlike behavior appeared again in Kristen.

Kristen was enjoying every minute of the game. She and Foster would talk about his teenaged years growing up playing point guard for his team. He even boasted about his three-point game that broke the school record. Foster was not much of a bragger but being in Bulls stadium and in this environment, he had no other choice.

Kristen found herself leaning on Foster's shoulder while sipping her white wine.

"Thank you so much for inviting me," Kristen spoke into Foster's ear.

"I'm glad you wanted to come," Foster responded.

"This has been an awesome experience," Kristen spoke.

The game got to intermission. A few more people came through the doors to shake hands with Foster and introduce themselves to Kristen. Kristen even overheard some onlookers that whispered, "What a stunning woman Foster has," or "Who is she?" or "Is she Foster's girlfriend?"

The help brought in some of Chicago's finest deep-dish pizza. Kristen found herself in what she presumed as being heaven on earth. The women that were there were drawn to Kristen. Everyone was so polite and trying to get close to the lady that seemed to be Foster's new girlfriend. Everyone knew how big Foster's status was as the CEO of the company, but Kristen still had not realize this truth yet.

Kristen did not put two and two together. She was so wrapped up in Foster's care that she was unaware to his status. She saw him for who he seemed to be: compassionate, kind, humble, gentle, and spontaneous—all of which is why Kristen was falling madly in love with Foster.

Finally, the game ended. The Chicago Bulls had trampled the other team to defeat! The shouts and chanting from the crowd came blaring through the stadium, and Kristen jumped in excitement to see Chicago win. She leaped into Foster's arms and kissed him tightly on the lips. Foster smiled through his compressed lips from Kristen and hugged her tightly with joy. The two were becoming one.

The stadium emptied in no time as the fans celebrated their victory in the streets with banners held high and jerseys that looked like a bloodbath had taken place. Kristen held on to Foster's arm tight and thanked him for the evening.

"Glad you had a good time, Kristen," Foster stated.

"Thank you for a wonderful evening," Kristen replied.

"Are you a Chicago Bulls fan now?" Foster chuckled.

"Are you kidding me?" Kristen replied. "I'm born for this now!"

The two ended the evening with a kiss. Kristen thanked Foster again for a wonderful evening full of excitement, joy, and wonder.

Kristen ran inside her apartment and met Cathy.

"How was the game?" Cathy asked.

"Wonderful!" Kristen replied. "We even had box seats!"

"You're kidding me?" Cathy replied.

"Nope," Kristen responded. "Foster is such a gentleman."

"Well, he definitely knows how to treat a woman," Cathy replied.

Kristen made her way into her room for the evening. After changing into her nightgown, she fell back supine on the bed and gazed into the sky. She soaked in all the charismatic love she was having for Foster, a man who she dreamed of all her life, one that would not just be with her but walk beside her. She pondered at all the steps leading up to meeting Foster: the nursing home, to the lavish dates, to getting her new job, and everything in between.

Kristen was quickly falling in love with Foster. And Foster was feeling the same as he found himself looking out of his apartment into the night sky. It was as if they were both seeing each other in their own homes from a distance. Making a connection through their emotions that soaked in all the love they were feeling for each other. This was true love. But it was more than that. It was two very different lives and backgrounds that were colliding together and becoming one. A beautiful, significant, unwavering love that no one could break.

Chapter

11

Foster and Kristen were like a perfectly placed key and lock. The two were intricately synchronized to one another. Their relationship was coming to a point where they both knew the seriousness in their togetherness.

Kristen still had not fully caught on to the fact that Foster was the big CEO of the company she worked for now, although she started speculating that he was living well above his means and the people he was aligned with were all upper class in their way of living. She just saw Foster for who Foster was to her—Mr. McDreamy.

* * * * *

Kristen had decided it was time to go home for one week as she was feeling homesick. It had been a long time since she'd been to Potomac. She thought this would be a good "cleansing of the mind" time where she could reflect on her life and where she was currently. She missed her mom. She missed the rusted windmills swirling in the air. She missed church events that she had once attended.

The next day, she announced that she would take one week's worth of vacation to go back home. She let Foster know that she needed to spend time with her family.

"Okay, if that's what you want to do," Foster spoke. "I support that."

"Yeah, nothing against you," Kristen returned. "I just need some time to think."

"Is there something I did?" Foster questioned.

"No!" Kristen replied. "I just miss my family."

"Well…" Foster stopped. "Wait! What if I tagged along with you?"

Kristen paused for a moment as she was in shock by Foster, a city boy, wanting to tap out of the city and come to her little farm town.

"I don't see why not?" Kristen replied.

"Then it's settled," Foster said. "I'm coming with you!"

Sure, he was charming and daring, but she had not seen the giddiness in his voice like this before. She wondered what his intentions were. *Is he wanting to lead her on? Keep her an arm's length away? Did he have something up his sleeve?* All these questions resonated within her mind. Nevertheless, the two of them were going to head to her hometown: Potomac, Illinois!

* * * *

The next week, the two of them had chosen to take his BMW all the way to Potomac, about 120 miles away. Foster had picked up Kristen at her apartment. Luckily, Foster didn't show up in a three-piece-suit. That would have been embarrassing.

On the flip side of things, he didn't dress in a flannel shirt and Wrangler jeans either. Thank God, that might have been the biggest impersonating move Foster had. Nonetheless, Foster showed up in a plain pair of shorts and a throwback Polo shirt. Kristen grinned at how cute Foster looked. What's even cuter is that Foster was childlike in his behavior on their adventure off to the country.

The two chatted all the way to Potomac as the sun hit their dark sunglasses gleaming into the sunset. It was only a couple hour's drive, but the conversation was endless. Kristen not only thought of Foster as Mr. McDreamy but as a man who was her best friend. For the moment, Kristen started to identify what true love was all about—romance and companionship.

Foster, in return, was taken in by Kristen's small-town spirit. He wondered what Kristen did in her little town. Was she the class clown, star cheerleader, or the awkward FFA president who immersed herself in farming? He even chuckled at thinking up that one.

Finally, Kristen and Foster pulled up to Kristen's mom's house. It was just as Foster thought. It was a tall, aged home with paint stripped off the shutters on the outside. The house was a two-tone color. It was a beautiful country house surrounded by cornfields.

Kristen was excited to meet her mother as she ran out the screened front door.

The two squeezed each other as if there would be no air left in either of them. They both chatted back and forth like two teenage girls at a sleepover.

Foster became a little uncomfortable because they almost forgot he was in their presence.

"I am so sorry, Mother," Kristen spoke. "This is my friend, Foster."

"Well, it's very nice to meet you, Foster!" Kristen's mother announced as she ran over to firmly shake Foster's hand.

Kristen's mother's hand was covered in flour, and she draped a quilted kitchen apron over her.

"Very nice to meet you, Leslie," Foster said.

What was intended to be a handshake went directly into to a glamorous hug. Foster was held like he was family, regardless of their relationship status. Kristen's mom was just the hugging type.

* * * * *

The day was spent catching up on small-town gossip, with Kristen learning about what had changed, who had broken up, who had kids, and any other nonsense gossip Leslie could get out. It was good for Kristen to be home. She almost forgot how quiet it was in the country life compared to the sirens and noise in the big city of Chicago. She was really drawn to both.

Kristen took Foster to see the livestock all throughout the farm. She showed him the different sheep, chickens, and horses she grew up around. Kristen always loved the animals on her backyard. She had that tender heart to take care of others.

"Let's go for a horseback ride, come on!" Kristen excitingly said.

"Sure," Foster responded.

The two got saddles and jumped willingly on the backs of her favorite horses. Honestly, Foster was a little apprehensive, but he was not there to be comfortable; he was there to show Kristen his submissive behavior and to be open to change.

The two rode off into the hills with the sunshine in their faces. Foster attempted to make some bold moves before he was put back in his place by her horse. Kristen laughed at his daring moves, but she knew none of his charm would work that well for Betsy. She admired his attempt though.

They both enjoyed each other's company, and the two seemed to draw closer and closer through new experiences together.

Foster's willingness to come and meet her family took their relationship to new heights. Foster was experiencing country life like no other. He even thought that he could be a country boy. Kristen made him never forget his day job. But what was happening through the visit to Potomac is that Kristen was falling madly in love with Foster.

Not once did she see a man get outside of his comfort zone for her. And never did she think that another man could ride Betsy so well. Foster, on the other hand, saw the genuineness and vibrancy in Kristen, something he never experienced with other women who only wanted him for what he represented—money.

Throughout the week, Foster had drippings of biscuits and gravy in his plate. He experienced how to collect eggs from the newly hatched chicks. He got to sit on the front porch and have endless conversations with Kristen without the distraction of his phone all day. This was not just a getaway for Kristen; this was a newfound glory for Foster just as much.

It showed Foster that life is short and money is temporary. What's important in life is being together with the people that make you smile and don't care how big your bank account happens to be. Life is about seeing and living every day as if tomorrow was never promised. That's what Foster's eyes were open to as he took this week to reflect on his own life.

On the last night, Kristen fell asleep on the sofa in Foster's arms. Foster lifted his arm and carried Kristen to the bedroom. He pulled the blankets over her shoulder. The moon was reflecting over her face. She was stunning and beautiful.

"Foster," Kristen quietly spoke.

"Yes," Foster replied.

"Don't ever leave me," Kristen said. "You are the best thing that has happened to me."

Foster smiled as he took a blanket and headed to the living room out of respect for Kristen. Foster pondered on how good he was feeling. He knew something magical was happening. And as his positive thoughts filled his mind, he drifted soundly off to sleep.

* * * * *

The next morning Kristen was awakened by Foster.

"Good morning," Foster said.

"Wow," Kristen replied. "What time is it?"

"It's ten a.m.," Foster responded.

Foster got up early with Leslie to help cook their last meal before he and Kristen hit the road to head back to Chicago. The week was filled with spontaneity. The random acts of kindness and farm living would be a week neither of them forget.

* * * * *

After breakfast, Foster overheard Leslie pleading with the local bank's loan officer, Darren, on the phone and asking for additional time in paying her loan. She was telling the loan officer that she'd had significant loss of income this year from a lack of rain. So their corn crop wasn't good because of the drought.

Foster noticed Leslie's helplessness and the anxiety on her face.

"I understand, ma'am, but there's just not any flexibility with the rules at our bank."

Foster wondered about what he could do to help solve Leslie's problem.

"Darren, I will come down to Hometown Bank tomorrow to discuss this with you on Friday," Leslie told Darren.

"Sure, ma'am," Darren said.

Foster told Leslie that he'd be back in a few minutes. He needed to go the store and get some shaving cream.

"Sure, Foster," Leslie said.

Foster drove to Hometown Bank to meet with Darren.

"Hello, Darren, I'm Foster," Foster introduced himself. "May I speak to you in private?"

"Yes, sir," Darren replied as he escorted Foster with him into a cubicle and closed the door. "Please be seated."

"Thank you, Darren," Foster said.

"How may I help you, Foster?" Darren asked.

"I'm here to talk about Ms. Leslie's loan payment," Foster explained. "I'm a family friend. I overheard your conversation with Leslie. Do you mind to tell me the amount of the loan payment?"

"Well, it is $1,650, sir," Darren told Foster.

"I actually want to know the total amount of the principal loan," Foster explained.

Darren looked through his computer to find the specific details of the loan.

"Sir, it is $55,600," Darren stated.

"Well, will you take a check?" Foster asked.

"Yes, sir," Darren agreed.

Foster pulled out his checkbook and wrote the check for $55,600.

Darren was expecting a payment for just the regular monthly mortgage amount. So he was stunned to see a check for $55,600.

"Are you sure, sir?" Darren questioned Foster.

"Yes, Darren," Foster assured confidently.

"Would you like to have a water or soda, sir?" Darren asked Foster.

"I will have water," Foster said. "Thanks, Darren."

Darren rushed to his office and got a bottle of water from the fridge. Darren was in disbelief that someone that's just a family friend will pay off this loan. Never in his tenure as a banker had he seen such an act of kindness.

Foster told Darren to give the deed to Leslie.

"Sure, I will, Foster," Darren agreed.

Foster shook hands with Darren and said, "Thank you."

"You are welcome, sir," Darren said.

* * * * *

Foster arrived back at Leslie's house.

"Where did you go, Foster?" Kristen asked.

"I just stopped by the grocery store to get some shaving cream," Foster replied. "I forgot to bring it with me."

"Well, lunch will be ready soon," Kristen said.

"That's awesome, Kristen," Foster replied.

"I will take quick shower," Kristen told Foster.

Leslie was busy in the kitchen preparing lunch. But she is still nervous, while thinking about the mortgage payment. Kristen had gone to take her shower.

"Ma'am, could I speak to you for a moment out on the porch?" Foster asked Leslie.

"Sure, Foster," Leslie agreed.

"I just want to let you know that I spoke with Darren at Hometown Bank," Foster explained to Leslie. "And I paid off your mortgage loan. Darren is going to give you the deed papers on Friday."

"Oh my, Foster," Leslie exclaimed. "I don't know what to say."

Leslie just could not believe Foster's generosity in doing something like this.

"Foster, you didn't have to do that," Leslie insisted. "That's a lot of money."

"It's my pleasure, ma'am," Foster assured.

Leslie's hands were shaking. She held Foster's hands and said, "Thank you."

"Please don't ever tell Kristen about this," Foster insisted to Leslie.

"Sure, I won't, Foster," Leslie promised. "I give you my word on that."

As Foster and Leslie were talking, Kristen appeared and asked them what they were talking about.

"Nothing, Kristen," Foster said. "I was just telling your mom how beautiful it is in Potomac. And the entire town seems is like an extended part of your family."

"It's absolutely true, Foster," Kristen agreed wholeheartedly. "Well, I'm hungry. Let's eat."

"Sure, Kristen," Foster said.

"Give me a couple of minutes to arrange the dishes on the table," Leslie said.

"We'll help you, ma'am," Foster said.

Foster joined Kristen and Leslie to help arrange the dishes on the table. They sat down at the table, and Kristen said a prayer before they started eating.

Foster complimented Leslie for a delicious lunch.

"I've had a great time here in Potomac," Foster stated.

"Foster, you can come visit us any time," Leslie said.

"That's really nice of you, ma'am," Foster graciously replied. "Thank you."

∗ ∗ ∗ ∗ ∗

Unfortunately, everything has an end, and Foster and Kristen had to say goodbye to her mother. They gave their goodbye hugs and jumped into Foster's BMW. Leslie waved with both arms as the vehicle drove off in the distance. Kristen would not stop waving as she watched her mother shrink in the distance of her rearview mirror.

The two love birds chatted all the way home. They laughed, they joked with one another, and Kristen even brought up the embarrassing moment when Foster thought the rooster was going to lay an egg and chased him around the chicken coop. Regardless, love was something that could be tangibly felt in the air. The growth the two of them experienced would be the knitted solution they felt about each other.

Everything has an end though, an end to a great week. But a better view on where this relationship would take them next. Sometimes though there's always a thorn in the bush that tries to break things up.

Chapter

12

Something special happened back at Kristen's hometown. Never in a million years has Kristen seen someone so kind, so generous, so becoming of her that she was assured Foster might be the one. Kristen's perspective changed that week. Her focus changed. Her ambition changed. Her care for another man changed. True love is not just something that is acquired instantaneously, it builds over time. And for Kristen, her love for Foster grew more as the weeks and months went by.

However, a friend of Foster's, Kelly, from many years ago soon caused problems. Kelly happened to be in Chicago to launch a French perfume business. Not surprisingly, Kelly's parents called Foster to see if he has time to help Kelly. Of course, being such a nice guy, Foster agreed right away. So Kelly sent an email to Foster explaining that her business venture is with a US-based company in Chicago. Kelly informed Foster about her arrival date and time in Chicago. She had planned to stay with her aunt in Chicago.

Foster was at the office when he received a call from Kelly, reminding him of her arrival time in Chicago at 6:00 p.m.

"Glad you reminded me, Kelly," Foster said. "Yes, I will be there to pick you up, Kelly."

Foster had seen Kelly a few years ago when he was visiting London with his parents.

Kelly inquired about Foster and was very much impressed with his achievements. Having seen Foster's picture in a magazine and reading that he was one of the top under-thirty entrepreneurs in Chicago made Kelly attracted to him.

Foster made it to the airport right on time to get Kelly.

"Hello, Foster," Kelly said when she called him from inside the airport.

"I just landed. I just need to pick up my baggage. I will be out in few minutes."

"Sure, Kelly," Foster replied politely.

Kelly was wearing a beautiful outfit with glasses positioned over her forehead. She did look beautiful, and it was difficult to miss her in a crowd.

"Hello, Foster," Kelly said as she hugged him. "Thank you for coming to pick me up."

"Not a problem at all, Kelly," Foster stated. "How was your flight?"

"It was good, Foster," Kelly said.

"You haven't changed a bit, Kelly," Foster complimented her. "You look beautiful."

"Thank you, Foster," Kelly said graciously. "You look handsome."

"So how long you will be Chicago?" Foster asked Kelly.

"Maybe a month," Kelly speculated.

"How are your parents?" Foster asked.

"They are doing well, Foster," Kelly replied. "Thank you for asking."

As they approach Lake Shore Drive, Kelly said, "Wow, what a beautiful view."

"I've always loved Chicago," Foster said. "It's so vibrant and full of life. Yes, I do like Chicago a lot, Kelly."

"So I've wanted to hear your suggestions about launching this perfume business right here in the US," Kelly stated.

"Sure, Kelly," Foster replied.

"Can we meet this coming Saturday?" Kelly asked Foster.

"Sure, why not, Kelly?" Foster agreed.

"Ah, you are so nice," Kelly replied, holding Foster's hands softly. "You know, Foster, you were so quiet when you were in high school. Remember, Foster, you were in the top rank of your class all throughout high school."

"Ah, that's not a big deal," Foster told Kelly.

"Remember, you were my date at our senior year prom party," Kelly recalled. "It was a memorable one. Everyone thought our dance was the best."

"Yep, Kelly." Foster smiled. "So many beautiful memories to cherish."

Kelly was feeling good about Foster's reactions to their conversation.

Now Kelly's aunt was waiting for them.

"Hello Foster," Pam said.

"Hi, Miss Pam," Foster replied.

Pam is in her early seventies. She had lost her husband just a year ago. Seeing Kelly brightened her face.

"Hi, Kelly, how was your flight?" Pam asked.

"It was great, Auntie," Kelly replied.

Foster brought Kelly's baggage inside, and then he received a phone call from his office.

"I need to go, Kelly," Foster said.

"How about we meet at ten a.m. on Saturday morning to discuss my business launch?" Kelly suggested.

"Sure," Foster said.

Kelly hugged Foster and told him goodbye. Foster told Miss Pam goodbye as well. And Pam also acknowledged Foster.

On his way to the office, Foster reminisced his high school days. He thought about how the future had turned out for his high school classmates.

Foster's mom called him.

"Kelly's parents told us that she is visiting Chicago on business," Foster's mom said.

"Yes, Mom," Foster replied. "I picked her up at the airport and just dropped her off at her aunt Pam's house."

"It's been a long time since I last saw Kelly," Foster's mom remembered. "How is she doing, Foster?"

"She is doing well," Foster replied.

"How about Pam?" his mom asked.

"I think Miss Pam is still slowly recovering since her husband passed away," Foster responded.

"I know, Foster, it's difficult," his mom said. "But time is a healer."

"I agree, Mom," Foster said. "And they we're married for forty-five years."

"Foster, please see if you can make time to help Kelly," his mom requested.

"Sure, Mom, I will," Foster promised. He was just getting to the office. "I will call you this weekend. Love you, Mom."

* * * * *

The following Saturday, Foster got a call from Kelly.

"How are you, Foster?" Kelly asked.

"Doing well," Foster replied. "I'm coming to your place around ten a.m."

"Foster, that's sounds great," Kelly replied. "I am looking forward to hearing your thoughts, Foster, about launching my business in the US."

"Sure, Kelly," Foster said. "I will see you soon."

* * * * *

Foster pulled his car into the driveway. And Kelly was waiting for him. Before Foster could even ring the doorbell, Kelly opened the door.

"Wow, you are on time, Foster," Kelly said as she seemed surprised.

"Well, the traffic was light, given that today is Saturday," Foster explained.

"Would you like to have a cup of coffee?" Kelly asked.

"Sure," Foster agreed. "With sugar and cream."

"Yep," Kelly replied to Foster.

Foster walked into the study room.

"Just give me few minutes to get you coffee," Kelly stated. Kelly walked into the kitchen.

Foster smiled.

A little bit later, Kelly returned with two cups of coffee.

Foster sipped his coffee and said, "Wow, it tastes so good."

"Thank you," Kelly replied. "You should try my pasta, Foster. I think you'd really love it."

"Sure," Foster said. "I will do that, Kelly."

"Here is the plan for introducing the perfumes with the help of LA Beauty Parlors," Kelly explained. Kelly thoroughly covered her presentation.

Foster fired off several questions, such as what age group Kelly was targeting and if it would be ages eighteen to fifty. He also asked about the pricing. Kelly mentioned that she was thinking in the mid-range of current US prices.

Foster asked more key questions, including why customers should buy Kelly's products when there are so many options for buying perfumes and what makes her product so unique.

"Well, we have an excellent product line, and with it being made in France, that gets more attention," Kelly explained. "In addition, the leading lady advertising the product is a well-known Hollywood actress. She even got an Oscar for best supporting role in 2005."

"Wow, that's great," Foster replied. "I would suggest that you keep the price in the higher range to get it noticed. In addition, giving it higher margin for the LA franchise will help push your product out in the market."

"That sounds great, Foster," Kelly agreed. "I will run those ideas by my marketing team."

"Great, Kelly," Foster said.

"I was wondering if you could accompany me to New York this weekend?" Kelly asked. "But only if you are free."

Foster pauses, remembering the promise he made to Kelly's father.

"Let me check with my secretary," Foster said. "I will let you know on Monday."

"That's not a problem," Kelly stated. "We can spend some quality time together."

"I agree," Foster said.

Kelly remembered how both she and Foster's parents used to talk about how her and Foster were made for each other growing up.

"Oh, yeah." Foster also remembered. Foster really didn't know what else to say, so he just smiled.

But Kelly took it as if Foster agreed with that thought. They went back to their high school days, remembering all the funny things that they'd done together. They were laughing like little kids.

Pam walked into the room and said, "It looks like you guys are having fun."

"Yes, Miss Pam," Foster responded. "We were talking about all the crazy things we did back in high school."

* * * * *

Foster got a phone call from Kelly's dad after his meeting with her and he had requested that Foster escort his daughter to New York. He was worried about Kelly going to New York by herself.

"Sure, I will, Uncle," Foster committed to the request from Kelly's dad.

So Foster called Kelly and told her that he is free to go with her to New York.

"That sounds awesome, Foster," Kelly said. "I will book our flight."

* * * * *

Foster had been so busy with Kelly, he'd hardly had any time to spend with Kristen. In fact, he was deeply involved with a business venture that he'd been working on for the past two years. It would be a multimillion-dollar deal if it worked out. So between his business venture and working with Kelly, he hardly had time for anyone and anything else.

It was obvious that Kelly had intentionally kept Foster away from Kristen. As a matter of fact, Kelly was behaving as if Foster was her man. But Foster didn't say anything because he didn't want to hurt Kelly's feelings.

Kelly booked a hotel near Time Square for her and Foster. It was a five-star hotel overlooking Time Square. She booked business class flight tickets for them.

Foster picked up Kelly two hours before their flight was scheduled to depart. Kelly's aunt's home was just thirty minutes away from the airport. Foster opened the car door for Kelly, and she told him thank you and that he was such a gentleman. Kelly was wearing a beautiful Prada dress.

"You look beautiful in that dress Kelly," Foster complimented her.

"Thank you, Foster," Kelly said.

Kelly was falling in love with Foster. Of course, she was drawn toward his wealth more than anything.

It didn't take long to reach the airport. Foster parked the car after dropping Kelly off at their arrival gate. When Foster got inside, Kelly was holding on to his arm as they walked toward the gate. Being a gentleman, Foster didn't object.

"You remember, Foster, how our parents had always thought we should get married when we grew up," Kelly nudged Foster.

"I know, Kelly," Foster admitted. "But we were so young at the time those comments were made."

"But don't you think they were right," Kelly persisted.

Foster just smiled.

"This way, ma'am," the flight hostess said.

They were seated in business class.

"What would like to drink ma'am?" the flight hostess asked Kelly.

"White wine," Kelly replied.

"How about you, sir?" the flight hostess asked Foster.

"I will have the same," Foster responded.

"Thank you, Foster, for coming with me to New York," Kelly told Foster.

Kelly asked Foster about his long-term plans. Foster explained to Kelly that he wants to settle in Chicago since he's made so many friends there.

"I love Chicago any day," Foster said. "My business is doing very well, Kelly."

"I'd also love to live in Chicago, Foster," Kelly stated.

"That's nice, Kelly," Foster said.

Their flight departed on time. Kelly was resting her head on Foster's shoulder and gently holding his hands. She became like a giddy teenager, chatting away. At the same time, Foster ate his snacks and drank a few sips of wine. The air hostess announced that their flight is going to land in twenty minutes. So Kelly goes to the restroom to freshen up. Foster finished his wine before Kelly returned.

They took a cab to their hotel. Kelly had booked a single king-sized bedroom. It was on the twentieth floor. A hotel butler brought their baggage into the room. Foster slipped him a $10 tip. Soon after, Kelly talked Foster into going out for dinner. They had a great time at the restaurant, and their dinner was excellent.

By the time they got back to their room, they were both tired. Kelly changed into her silk pajamas. Foster decided to take quick shower before going to bed. But Kelly went to sleep before Foster finished showering. Foster laughed at how quickly Kelly had fallen asleep, and he thought that it must've been a sugar coma from their dessert.

* * * *

The next morning, Kelly woke up early since she had a meeting with her client at the same hotel restaurant. She told Foster she'd ordered room service for his breakfast.

"No worries, Kelly," Foster said. "I will take care of it."

"By the way, Foster, I booked a Broadway show for tonight," Kelly surprised Foster.

"Wow, that's great, Kelly." Foster thanked her.

* * * *

Kelly returned to their hotel room around 4:00 p.m. She called Foster to find out where he was at. He happened to be in the lobby checking emails.

"Shall we go for dinner before heading to the Broadway show?" Kelly asked Foster.

"Sounds great," Foster replied.

"I heard there is a famous Italian restaurant a block from our hotel," Kelly suggested. "Shall we go there, Foster?"

"Sure," Foster said. "I will get ready in few minutes. I will come up soon."

After having dinner, they both went to the theater to see the Broadway show.

"Don't you think our dinner was great, Foster," Kelly stated.

"Yep, it was," Foster replied to Kelly.

The Broadway show they saw was *Phantom of the Opera*. It was an awesome performance by everyone.

"I loved it very much," Kelly said. "It was a great experience. Love is eternal and unconditional."

"Thank you for booking such a nice show, Kelly," Foster said politely.

"You're welcome, Foster," Kelly replied.

It was 11:00 p.m. by time they got back to the hotel. Now Kelly thought the time was right, and she wanted to make love with Foster. But Foster told Kelly that it wasn't appropriate for this because he'd given her father his word to watch out for her.

"Come on, Foster," Kelly tried to persuade Foster.

"I mean it, Kelly," Foster insisted.

"You are such a nice guy, Foster," Kelly said.

So she kissed him and said good night.

They flew back to Chicago the next day.

* * * * *

Foster had asked Kristen to join him for lunch a few weeks after coming back from Potomac. He was busy with office work and couldn't go out with Kristen. But this time, Foster had brought someone with him when they met at a restaurant during lunch hour.

Kristen was with her office colleague, Crystal. Kristen saw the woman from a distance. She could see her wearing high-end clothing and Prada glasses. She screamed money. She was also carrying a Louis Vuitton purse. She was very flashy in appearance.

"Kristen, meet my childhood friend, Kelly," Foster introduced.

"Hello, Kelly," Kristen replied.

"Hi there, Kristen," Kelly spoke. "I've heard a lot about you."

The appearance of Kelly didn't sit well with Kristen. She felt a bit intimidated by her, the way she made her feel little in front of Foster. Don't get the girl wrong, she was gorgeous as well. So for the first time, Kristen felt as though maybe Foster had hidden relationships, although she couldn't be certain in her assumptions. Kelly asked Kristen whether they would like to join them. Kristen said they were almost done eating lunch.

"We will meet again, Kristen," Kelly said.

"Sure, Kelly. I will get your cell number from Foster."

Kristen felt her mood change very quickly. She felt flashbacks from her past relationships stir up inside and had a sense of hopelessness.

"Are you okay?" Crystal asked.

"Nothing, Crystal," Kristen replied.

"Something seems wrong," Crystal continued.

"I'm fine," Kristen replied. "Let's eat."

Crystal insisted that she was going to buy Kristen's lunch. They talked about meaningless topics like recent favorite movies they had watched, although Kristen had difficulty concentrating or even holding on to a conversation.

"Oh, it's almost time to go to back to the office," Crystal interrupted.

"Time must have gotten away from us!" Kristen replied.

* * * * *

Kristen's mind was preoccupied over Kelly being with Foster and holding on to his arm, and she couldn't concentrate at work.

Kristen quickly exited from the office just after putting away daily activities at her desk. She hit the subway station to catch the train on time. Luckily, Kristen was able to squeeze in a spot at the back corner of the train.

Kristen did not feel well. She had this quivering motion in her stomach, like she was going to vomit. She took a few sips of water and downed a peanut butter candy bar. Her emotions were becoming physical, as though something was really wrong.

She gazed at the lighting coming off the train tracks. Her mind was racing and raging, both at the same time. If this was an intuition she was having about Foster, she had these before from past relationships that did not turn out well. Reluctantly, she wanted to hope for the best.

The train ride home made her think of Potomac, Illinois. She could see the countryside reflect off the tracks as they panned across the flooring outside her window. She recalled the loss of Michael to another woman, which resulted in the breaking of her engagement with him. Practically all the failures Kristen endured over the past months and years started piling up in the emotions she was having about Foster.

It's not that Kristen felt lost. More so, she felt that there would be no future with her for love—true love that is.

But there was something dangling in the atmosphere that was creating an uncertain, discomforting mood for Kristen. It was a woman who gave her a sour taste in her mouth, a woman who she had just recently met—Kelly.

Kelly wanted Foster. Badly. She wanted him not for his looks or his charm; she wanted him for his money. Kelly was a leech of a different breed. She gripped on to men who are steeped in success. Although Kristen didn't quite grasp that he was lavishly wealthy, Foster was targeted by Kelly just for that very reason. She wanted him and would push anyone out of the way who seemed to be a threat. Kristen was that threat.

Kelly happened to contact her once again when she dropped by at her workplace. And Kristen became childlike curious.

"How long have you known Foster?" Kristen asked her.

"Oh, I have known him since high school," Kelly replied.

So for a moment, Kristen felt better since they were just high school friends.

But Kelly sneakily always wanted Foster because he was a prince charming ever since a teenager. The conversation continued.

"I met Foster about two years ago when he visited me at a rehabilitation center," Kristen announced. "He visited me when he came and saw his aunt."

"So you mean he's just a friend?" Kelly insinuated.

"Yes, you can say that," Kristen responded. "He kept in touch with me since then. Why do you ask?"

"Oh, just asking," Kelly quickly responded.

So the two of them grew up in high school together but Foster never had any feelings for Kelly and still doesn't. Foster saw them as just friends. He cherished their friendship, so he never wanted to lead Kelly on.

Kelly, however, came to Chicago because she thought Foster still loved her, and she sought this moment to capture his attention. Kelly was an Oxford graduate with an MBA. She was witty, intelligent, and had mad drive. She was well accomplished in whatever she touched. She thought of success as a way of life, and Foster reeked of success, so this made him even more attractive.

"How about you come over to my place tonight?" Kelly asked.

"Sure, what time?" Kristen replied.

"How about six p.m.?" Kelly responded.

"Sounds good," Kristen replied.

* * * * *

Kelly texted Kristen the address to her home. She was staying at her uncle's mansion in the suburbs. Once Kelly did not feel that Kristen was a threat to taking Foster, she backed off a little. But Kelly was going to try and make sure Kristen believed Foster wanted her more than anything.

Kristen arrived, and they sat and drank a cool glass of wine together to lighten the mood. Kristen was curious about Kelly's Oxford studies and asked questions throughout the night about it. Kelly confidently boasted about her credentials and began to open up about how close Foster and her families were to each other. This uncomfortably didn't sit well with Kristen. It was intended to be a dagger by Kelly to Kristen's heart.

Kelly continued to drive the dagger deeper.

"Why, yes, Foster's parents used to joke about how we were to get married one day when we grow up," Kelly continued. "Foster is a wonderful guy, and I love him dearly."

That was it, the bullet that was the kill shot. Suddenly, Kristen felt this knot grow in her stomach. She had pain, sharp pain. This manifested as a sadness deep within Kristen's heart, and she felt as though Kelly would soon be Foster's girl.

Kelly could see the sorrow on her face and smirked devilishly. It was what Kelly intended to do. She wanted to annihilate Kristen out of the picture.

"Tell me more about yourself?" Kelly asked.

It took everything in Kristen's power to conjure up an answer. But through a large gulp in her throat, she managed to spit something out.

"I'm from Potomac," Kristen softly spoke. "It's a small town where everyone knows everyone."

"Wow, Potomac!" Kelly responded.

"Yeah, it's a small community," Kristen responded.

"I don't know what Foster saw in you," Kelly mumbled.

"Did you say something?" Kristen questioned.

"No, nothing at all," Kelly responded. "Just thinking how you have managed living in a big city."

"It was definitely a shock getting used to it," Kristen replied.

Kelly started to realize that Kristen had no idea how rich Foster really was at all. She was in no rush to tell Kristen any hidden secrets that might give her an advantage. As for Kelly, she was playing offense, and the defense for Kristen was slowly fading away.

"By the way," Kelly stated. "Sorry about your wreck."

"Thank you," Kristen replied. "Time heals all things."

"It surely does," Kelly insinuated.

Time seemed to be running out for Kristen. She was now face-to-face with her opponent. Kristen was never the aggressive type, but for some reason she felt competition stirring up deep within her soul. I suppose that's how you can tell when you're madly in love. Protection and ambition seem to come out of the unknown.

"By the way," Kelly stated. "We were at Foster's house yesterday." Kelly went on to tell Kristen they just had a small get-together. She boasted about how much fun the families had. How they got caught up on the past and talked about their high school friendship. Kelly not only was driving the nail, she was trying to take out the whole board. "In fact," Kelly went on. "I stayed with Foster all night talking about our childhood together." Kelly showed pictures where she was sitting in Foster's lap, kissing him on his cheek.

Kristen went from sadness to built-up anger and frustration. She could feel her face flush and steam coming from both her ears. She lost Michael to another woman, and she didn't want to lose Foster to this prodigy.

Kristen swallowed her pride, however, and chose to take a different tactic. Like a lioness, she waited for the right moment to take her prey. Kelly was now her opponent. She no longer saw her as someone who would come across as meek and genuine. Instead, she saw her as a threat and dangerous. She knew now that this meeting was an attempt to drown her out of the equation and make Foster her prize. In no way, shape, or form would Kristen go down lightly.

The night progressed, and both of them were exhausted. Kristen saw herself out the door and Kelly snake-eyed her out of the room. The two were antagonists to one another. Kelly felt like she won this battle, but Kristen felt like the war had just begun.

* * * * *

Shortly after Kristen left, she attempted to call Foster but there was no answer. She called again. Nothing. She worried about what happened back at Kelly's house. She had mixed emotions of uncertainty and discontentment. Part of her wanted to flat out ask Foster about Kelly and their plans, but something inside her felt that what was intended to be will be.

Kristen traveled home and shut her phone off for the night. Foster saw his missed calls from her and tried several times to call her back. But it went straight to voice mail. He wanted to leave a voice mail but felt it would be best to try again tomorrow.

* * * * *

The next morning, when Kristen opened her phone, she saw no missed calls from Foster. Things got real now. She knows Foster likely saw her missed calls and chose to not call her back.

What is going on? Does Foster really care for Kelly? Have I been misled once again by someone who I cared about? Questions started to turn to fears.

Kristen felt déjà vu when she visually saw her relationship with Foster fall apart. Kristen had seen this pattern before.

That day Kristen traveled back to work by train. She went to her regular cubical and couldn't get her personal life off her brain. There was no sign of Foster either. She was uncertain what really was going on between them two.

Suddenly, Kelly showed up.

"What are you doing?" Kelly asked.

"Just getting ready for the day," Kristen replied.

"Have you talked to Foster?" Kelly instigated.

"Not yet," Kristen responded.

"I talked to him last night after you left," Kelly stated.

Kelly had devilishly talked to Foster after Kristen left and gave him about all kinds of false information spoken during their visitation. Foster was confused of what Kelly said of Kristen's disinterest in Foster and how Kristen was looking into dating other men.

"What did he say?" Kristen questioned.

"Nothing about you," Kelly responded. "We just talked about how our day went."

Now Kristen's doubts seemed to increase in the confirmation that Kelly and Foster were destined to be together. She almost felt numb to the situation. The feelings for Foster seemed to fade away. Not because Kristen was falling out of love with him, that would never change, but that she had to let him go.

Kelly was such an instigator. She was prude, deceptive, and flat-out evil. Even the staff at the office could smell her from around the corner. The employees there knew about Kelly and her devices. They dared not tell Kristen about anything because they didn't know what other tactics Kelly had up her sleeves and whether she would gossip about them to Foster. So everyone just stayed to their business.

* * * * *

Things started to change around the office. Kristen was becoming quiet. She was becoming isolated. Depression and anxiety were filling her life. Kristen didn't know what to do next. She was coming to a point in her life where either she was going to leave her job or find a way to swallow her defeat with Kelly.

Kristen left work that evening heavyhearted. She had lost hope and decided to go home briefly. She wanted to take some time off. She told Cathy about her conversations with Kelly. Cathy tried to console her but failed. Cathy told Kristen that it wasn't a bad idea to take a break. So, with the following day being a Friday, Kristen called the office about taking a leave for one day. She drove to Potomac on Friday morning.

* * * * *

Leslie was surprised to see Kristen coming without telling her. But she was happy to see her daughter. Her grandparents were also happy. Kristen was the center of attention of the whole family as she was adored by her nieces and nephews. They had great a lunch and dinner, reminiscing old memories.

The following day, Leslie and Kristen went to a local shop to buy some groceries.

Kristen's high school classmate, Austin, noticed Kristen at the store. Austin had a crush on Kristen in high school but never dared to tell her.

"Hi, Kristen," Austin said. "You are looking good, Kristen."

"Thank you," Kristen replied.

Austin told Kristen she hadn't changed much. Kristen told Austin the same.

"I heard that you are working in that big city of Chicago," Austin said to Kristen.

"Yep, Austin," Kristen confirmed. "Things are going well so far."

"That's good, Kristen," Austin applauded.

"How about you?" Kristen asked Austin.

Austin replied, "I'm working as a banker at our local hometown bank."

"Oh, that's exciting," Kristen politely replied.

"Anyway, I was wondering whether you are free tomorrow to go out for dinner?" Austin asked Kristen.

"Sure, Austin," Kristen agreed.

"I will pick you at seven p.m.," Austin confirmed.

Kristen just couldn't say no to Austin.

Kristen's mom watched the interaction with Austin from a distance. Seeing the smile on Kristen's face made Leslie happy.

On their way home, Leslie said, "Wow, Austin turned out to be a gentleman."

"You are right, Mom," Kristen agreed. "He asked me to go out for a dinner tomorrow."

"Did you say yes?" Leslie asked.

"Yep," Kristen replied quickly.

Leslie told Kristen that Austin comes from a nice family. Kristen told her mom that she knew that. Of course, Leslie was hoping that Kristen would like Austin.

* * * * *

So Kristen went to dinner with Austin the following day. He picked Kristen up right on time and told her she looked beautiful. Kristen thanked Austin for the compliment and told him that he looked sharp as well. Austin smiled at Kristen. They reminisced about their high school days while laughing their hearts out about all the things they did.

Austin asked Kristen if she is seeing anyone. She told Austin that she wasn't seeing anyone and that after the setback with her engagement, she'd never seriously thought of dating again just yet. Austin told Kristen he understood and that he was sorry for her.

"How about you, Austin?" Kristen asked.

"I dated couple of girls but nothing worked out," Austin replied.

"Sorry to hear that, Austin," Kristen sympathized.

"No worries," Austin replied. "There is always someone out there, and we will find them when the time is right."

"You are very philosophical, Austin," Kristen stated.

"Well, life teaches us lessons, Kristen," Austin suggested.

"You are right," Kristen agreed.

Kristen and Austin chatted away and had a great time revisiting their high school days. They thanked each other for a wonderful dinner and for catching up on high-school memories. After getting back to Leslie's house, Austin opened the car door for Kristen, smiled at her, told her goodbye, and gave her a hug.

That night Kristen's mom and grandparents were in favor of Kristen marrying Austin. Kristen told her mom she didn't think that was the right thing to do. Kristen's mom informed her that she had gotten a call from Austin's parents. Kristen's grandparents also interjected that they wanted to see her get married before they died. Kristen told her grandparents not to talk about leaving her and that she loved them more than anything. She had tears in her eyes that overflowed to her cheeks.

She wiped her tears away and promised to think about marrying Austin. Kristen's mom and grandparents liked that answer and told her she didn't have to say anything right away because Austin will wait for her.

Kristen went to her room, pondering the idea of getting married to Austin. But she loved Foster so much that she couldn't think of living without him in her life.

Leslie walked into Kristen's bedroom and sat on the bed. Kristen put her head in her mom's lap and broke down. She told her mom that she loved Foster very much and couldn't stop crying.

Kristen's mom comforted her and told her not to cry. Kristen told her mom that any girl would say yes to Foster. She told her mom that Foster is handsome and kind and knows how to take care of a woman. She told her mom how he was there every time she needed help after her accident and how he treated her so nicely and took time off from his busy schedule to be with her. She also told her mom that he had never once hurt or mistreated her.

Kristen said she knew she was being selfish when it came to Foster, but that he deserved the best life partner, although she doubted whether she'd be that women in his life. Kristen wondered if Kelly happened to be the right woman for him because she is rich, Oxford trained, and beautiful. Kristen told her mom that her heartache was difficult to bear for her right now.

Kristen's mom said, "God has plans for us, and we will leave this to Him."

Kristen agreed with her mom.

Kristen was mumbling and dozed off to sleep. Kristen's mom told her not to worry and that everything would be all right, then she kissed her forehead.

* * * * *

Later, Kristen woke up to her mom's voice, telling her she has a call from Foster.

Kristen jumped out of bed and shouted that she'd pick up the phone.

"Hello, Kristen," Foster said. "How are you?"

"I'm doing well, Foster," Kristen replied. "I was trying to call your cell, but it was going to voice mail."

"I got your home phone number from Cathy. What happened? You left without even mentioning."

"Well, I was feeling home sick, so I thought of coming down to Potomac," Kristen explained to Foster.

"I can understand, Kristen," Foster stated.

Kristen didn't want to tell Foster that she had told Kelly to inform him about her going to Potomac. She realized Kelly didn't convey her messages to Foster.

"Hope you are feeling better now," Foster told Kristen.

"Yep, Foster," Kristen replied.

"By the way, I'm throwing a party at my place this coming weekend," Foster mentioned. "I would like you to be there."

"Sure, Foster," Kristen agreed. "How can I miss your party?"

"I love that answer, Kristen," Foster said excitedly. "By the way, I invited Cathy and she said yes too."

Kristen's heart started beating faster. She was happy to hear Foster's voice. It was a day and night difference in her mood. Kristen's mother asked her if everything was okay.

Kristen told her mom that everything was good and that Foster had invited her to a party at his home this coming weekend.

Kristen packed her stuff the next day. She said goodbye to her mother and grandparents, gave them hugs, and headed back to Chicago. Kristen's mom told her to drive safely. She told her mom she would and that she'd call her once she got to her apartment.

* * * * *

Kristen reached Chicago around 6:00 p.m. She arrived, and Cathy could tell something was up.

"You, okay?" Cathy asked.

"Yeah," Kristen responded. "Just a long drive."

"Well, I made dinner," Cathy replied.

The two sat and had a long conversation about Foster and their future. Kristen told Cathy about everything. Cathy wanted to go to battle with Kristen, but she pushed her off and calmed her down.

Cathy encouraged Kristen that everything was going to be okay and that she should fight for her prize.

Kristen agreed but had no idea how to approach Foster about the situation. Nevertheless, Kristen felt that Foster's upcoming party would be the moment she would tell him everything. Yeah, Kristen was going to put her best suit on and party like she has never partied before.

Chapter

13

The whole workforce knew about Foster's big party. From the moment Foster invited Kristen, it was a constant conversation piece, spread throughout her workplace. Kristen happened to be a little thrown off that Foster's house was building up so much buzz, and she became alert to the fact that Foster must be someone or somebody she hadn't realized before.

Kristen pranced home after getting her ruby-red dress for the night. Cathy even dressed up a bit to her surprise and ran into the living room with an eloquent violet dress. The two even synchronized their dance recital for the evening. Cathy had a heavy foot though. Her balance appeared a bit off in her high heels.

Cathy flattened herself on the hardwood floor, and Kristen burst out into laughter. Cathy even allowed Kristen to chuckle at her flaws since it had been days since Cathy saw Kristen's smile. She had built up a tower of tears from the previous days because of Kristen's broken heart. But Kristen made a deal with herself that she would be happy for Foster, even if it was with another woman. Kristen thought real love needs sacrifice. Kristen love for Foster was unconditional.

Kristen thought that she had something special with Foster, but through her discernment, she quickly realized he likely had eyes for Kelly. Nevertheless, true love allows the ones you cherish to find their own path, whatever the outcome may be.

The two dashed into Cathy's vehicle and headed to Foster's home.

* * * *

They pulled up to Foster's traditional midcentury mansion. It was made of stone with vaulted towers throughout and tucked away nicely on a hill for the entire city to see. Cathy was wowed by its appearance. There were high-profile cars wrapped around the pull-through driveway. There was even valet parking.

They were welcomed by butlers at the front door and given matching champagne as an introductory gesture. There was a pianist tucked in the corner playing rhythmic music to match the motion of the people. The night was perfect. The mansion was filled to the brim with people all decked out in fashionable dresses and tuxedos. Kristen was blown away by the makeup of the evening.

Kristen brought a small present and card for Foster. Secretly, it was a fountain pen.

Foster noticed Kristen and Cathy immediately as they arrived.

"Ladies," Foster announced.

"Why, hello, Foster," Cathy replied. "Now this is a party!"

"I'm glad you both came." Foster smiled.

"Yes, we are glad to be here," Kristen replied.

"I hope that you two enjoy yourselves," Foster responded. "It's going to be a magical night."

How Kristen adored this man. She saw herself walking down the aisle with him. She saw herself having children with him. She saw herself getting old with him. But deep within her heart, it was aching, driven by the pain of another woman who took him from her.

There was something about Kristen though. She had humility built up in her and compassion for others that no person could ever get away from. She was happy for Foster, no matter what his future portrayed.

"You look beautiful, Kristen," Foster continued.

"And you look quite handsome yourself," Kristen replied.

"Well, you two enjoy, I'll see you hear shortly," Foster said.

"Sounds wonderful," Kristen closed.

Kristen's eyes had been a little red from the previous nights. She applied extra makeup so that Foster couldn't see her trauma. She hadn't slept well either.

Even during the night, Kristen reflected on her time with Foster. How she spent so much time with him and the closeness of his touch. He never hurt or harmed her. He was genuine in all his ways.

Suddenly, Kristen wasn't feeling so good. Her eyes grew larger. She began to sweat and feel a bit dizzy.

"Are you okay?" Cathy asked.

"Yes," Kristen replied. "I just need a glass of water."

"No," Cathy responded. "You don't look so good."

"I'm all right," Kristen replied.

Cathy saw Kristen's color grow even paler. She was as white as a ghost and found herself off balance. Cathy and another woman grabbed Kristen and dragged her into one of the bedrooms. The room was larger than her whole house back at Potomac. Cathy turned the lights low and laid Kristen on the bed.

The other woman grabbed a glass of water and gently placed it against Kristen's lips.

"I'm feeling better," Kristen spoke.

"I'm worried about you, Kristen," Cathy stated. "Maybe we should head home?"

"No, no. I'll be fine," Kristen announced.

The three of them walk gently out of the room back to the party. As they made their way back into the large room, the music started to fade out. An announcement was made to shush the crowd.

"Everyone, Foster would like to make an announcement."

The entire crowd, full of consultants and businessmen, some of the high-profile people, stared as Foster entered the room. He was dressed to impress, wearing a Gucci tuxedo that was custom made for this night.

The crowd was pushed aside as Foster began walking in the direction of Kristen. Now Kristen was in a trance seeing her prince prowl across the people. She saw Kelly in her view as well. This was the moment. She could tell Foster was about to propose to Kelly. How she longed to be the woman on the other side of the ring.

Foster was slowly making his way across the room as it appeared he was approaching Kelly. And Kelly had smile that resembled winning the lottery. After all, that's what she wanted in Foster, his wealth. But Foster kept walking. Kelly was appalled as Foster quickly walked right past her.

Kristen was confused as Foster walked by Kelly. Now he was making his way toward Kristen. She could feel her heartbeat in her throat. Foster's smirk resembled that he had something different up his sleeve.

He now was right in front of Kristen. He gently grabbed one of her hands.

"Kristen," Foster said, "ever since I met you, I knew you were special. We have grown so close over these past months and into the year, and I couldn't see myself with anyone else. I have seen you just as you are."

Foster continued, "You didn't know I was the CEO of this company. Not once did you want me for my money or my status. I can see myself with you forever."

Kristen was grabbing her chest at this moment. She was trying to slow down her breathing and retain everything that was being spoken to her.

And in this moment, this very moment, Kristen's life would be forever changed as she saw Foster get down on one knee.

"Kristen," Foster stated, "will you marry me?"

The whole room was shocked. If you could have taken a picture of the moment, everyone's mouths would be wide open. Everyone knew this was an engagement party, but they thought Kelly was the chosen girl.

"But," Kristen responded, "I thought you wanted to marry Kelly?"

"Kelly?" Foster replied. "She is just a good friend, always has been."

"I had no idea," Kristen said. "I just…"

"Kristen, you're the girl for me," Foster replied. "I want to spend forever with you. I have finally found my true love."

Kristen's tears welled up from within as joy hit the surface. "Yes! Yes!" Kristen shouted. "Yes! I will marry you!"

Foster lifted up Kristen aggressively as she built up involuntary strength from within and laid the biggest kiss on Foster. The crowd cheered and shouted.

Kelly, meanwhile, was infuriated. Her parents, who were invited by Kelly, were confused. Kelly stormed out the front door as she pushed every soul out of the way in disgust.

Kristen had won the war. She got her man. The two turned toward the crowd and waved as champagne flowed into every glass by the butlers and confetti filled the air. It was like being at Disney during the grand finale.

Cathy jumped into the arms of Kristen and felt so much happiness for her best friend. She knew Kristen's heart belonged to Foster, and she couldn't be more satisfied to see Foster propose.

"I am so, so happy for you two!" Cathy shouted.

"Thank you so much, Cathy," Kristen replied. "You have been the best during this!"

"And, Foster," Cathy spoke, "take care of my girl."

"I sure will," Foster replied. "You can count on it."

What a night. What a surprise. Kristen reminisced on her childhood when she would dream of this moment. A small girl in a small town who desperately wanted to find her husband one day. And today was just that—a genuine gentleman swept her off her feet. Sure, things appeared different for a minute; but in the end, through trials and hardships with other relationships, she found the one who would complete her.

The music came back on, and the dancing filled the night. People came up from everywhere congratulating the newly engaged couple. Kristen called her mother. Her mom was astonished and was excited for the news.

The night was like a blur for the two of them. They danced, they drank, and soon, they would be married.

You could have called this night true love, where two people found each other through hardship and suffering. Selflessly, each one cared so much for one another that they were willing to let each other go. True love is patient. It is kind and thoughtful. It is not jealous or envious of others. It never ever brags about what it has or does not have. It does not seek its own. True love rejoices over the wins, even the losses. It bears all things, believes all things, and hopes for all things.

That was Kristen's and Foster's relationship. A magical oneness. A complete equation to finding joy and peace within one another. It's obvious that true love still exists today, because as we know, love never fails.

Now comes the fun part. We have a wedding to plan!

Chapter

14

Word quickly got out that Foster and Kristen were engaged. The news spread faster than any rumor mill. It was at the front of every conversation and on the headlines of every newsstand. In fact, the *Chicago Tribune* newspaper headlined it, "Foster Got His Girl!"

Things didn't change for Kristen however. She was in love, and the recognition she was getting didn't fit her character. She was genuine, modest, and flat head over heels in love with her man.

Foster was the same: collective, charming, and humble. The glitz and glamour didn't bother Foster because he was born to be recognized.

Things moved quickly for the newly engaged couple. Aside from the size of the ring Foster placed on her finger, Kristen had a team that was ready to make her day spectacular. Assisted by a wedding planner, makeup artist, flower designer, and logistics team, Kristen was wooed by recognition.

"I hope this is not too much," Foster spoke.

"Well…" Kristen paused. "No, it's perfect!"

Foster laughed at the grimace on Kristen's face. She kind of looked like a cartoon character, with hearts inserted over her eyes as she gazed into the eyes of her man. Foster could tell that Kristen was obviously in love.

There was much to be done for this wedding. They were calling it the wedding of the decade. There was no getting by Kristen anymore. Noticing Foster as the CEO of his large corporation, it embarrassed Kristen that she didn't see it before. Even more so though, it revealed that love doesn't come with a price. Kristen loved Foster for who he was as an individual. This is something no money could buy.

Foster's parents were ecstatic. They loved Kristen and especially the very fact that she was a girl from a small town, rooted in integrity. Kristen's mother was overwhelmed. She was taking in all the wedding planning and how much Kristen stepped into the "new league." But Kristen's mother was still happy.

All of Foster's friends were cheering for him. They cherished Kristen for her divine, naturalistic Southern charm. And to be honest, the only person still sitting in her corner and sulking was Kelly. She was nowhere to be found. The night of the proposal, she hightailed it out of town and drove back home angry, betrayed, and ashamed.

However, there was one thing that seemed to bother Kristen. She was wondering who would walk her down the aisle. Kristen chose her grandfather to walk her down the aisle. But in the back of her mind, she always wanted her own father to do his duty. As a young girl, she dreamed of walking down the aisle in her lacy white attire. She tried to draw up any memory of her father growing up, but the vision never came into play. She didn't dare ask her mother about her father, as this conversation came up several times growing up and it never went anywhere.

The weeks went by, and the details were all coming together. She said yes to the dress! It was an elongated, lightly laced white dress that draped over her shoulders. She chose a crystal necklace to match the dress. She picked it up at the finest wedding store in Chicago. You needed reservations just to get in this store and were required to have a bank account that backed it up.

The flower bouquets that went on every table were the size of a small crape myrtle tree. Not to mention the ten thousand flowers that were assorted beautifully around the assembly, including the wedding chapel and reception tent.

Everything was set into motion, and the wedding day was here. It was time for the bride and groom to lock arms.

* * * * *

It is finally the wedding day. All the guests had arrived on time in their limousines and high-profile cars, while also dressed to the gills in black attire tuxedos and colorful dresses. Crystal was the theme women wore on this special day.

The wedding place was breathtaking. It was decorated magnificently and fit for a princess. Everyone was oohing and aahing at all the eye candy that they are seeing.

Kristen was tucked away in the dressing room. She was surrounded by women who were there to serve her. Foster's sister was in the room. Kristen's mother was at her side for every beck and call. The wedding dress, designed by a famous fashion designer, lay perfectly on the bed.

The women helped Kristen get into her dress without messing up her makeup.

"Oh, wow," Foster's sister stated. "You look so beautiful."

"Yes," Foster's mother announced. "Absolutely stunning."

"Thank you, guys," Kristen replied.

But suddenly, as Kristen was seeing herself in her wedding dress, she burst into tears. The women stopped and paused. No one knew what was going on in Kristen's mind.

"Are you okay?"

"What's wrong?"

"Do you not like the dress?"

These remarks came from the ladies in the room with her. Kristen's mother tried soothing her but to no avail. Kristen sobbed and sobbed. She had desperately wanted her father to be at her wedding. She had longed for his appearance.

Kristen didn't know what to do or how to get herself together, so she called John. She knew Foster had invited John, so she called him.

* * * * *

John was happy that his daughter was getting married to such a nice person like Foster, who is just so perfect and, above all, he's a gentleman. He wondered whether Kristen would ever forgive him for what he had done. He had an empty feeling in his stomach. He wished he'd gotten treatment for his alcohol and drug addiction much earlier. But he realized he couldn't change the past. So what will Kristen say about her father? Who would be walking Kristen down the aisle? His heart was beating faster, and his forehead was sweating. Never had a day gone by that he didn't think about his wife and daughter. He had been completely lost in his thoughts when his cell phone rang. It was Leslie. Her voice was in distress.

"Can you come into the dressing room quickly?" Kristen asked John on the phone.

"Yes," John replied. "I'll be right there."

The girls continued to comfort Kristen until John knocked on the front door.

"What's going on, Kristen?" John asked.

"It's…it's just…," Kristen replied through her tears. "I wanted my father to walk me down the aisle."

Suddenly the room got very quiet. Kristen's mother and John locked eyes.

"I think it's time," Kristen's mother announced.

John pulled up a seat and sat directly in front of Kristen.

"Kristen," John slowly said, "there is something I need to tell you."

Kristen stopped crying and gave John her full attention. John opened up about the time they met when he was "homeless." How he was an undercover agent and working as an informant. He remembered that he'd coincidentally pulled over Foster the night of her hospitalization for gastrointestinal bleeding.

Kristen, still in shock, kept listening.

"I met your mother when she was visiting you at the hospital the day after your hospitalization for gastrointestinal bleeding. I was looking for the right moment. Kristen"—John paused again—"I am your father."

The whole room gasped. Kristen practically fell over. John caught her before she collapsed to the ground.

You see, when Kristen was a little girl, John struggled with alcohol. He was in the military and had a lot of traumatic experiences that drove him to drink. He tried to quit. He wanted to be involved in her life. But he had to deal with his own mental health and how it was affecting his family and his marriage, so he left. He was lured into drinking even more and losing touch with reality before finally getting help.

John was ashamed. He joined the police academy and accomplished something good with his life but could not draw up the courage to come back home and give Kristen the dad she deserved.

So, being curious about Kristen during her adulthood and while they are both living in Chicago, John kept an eye on his daughter to help protect her. He showed up but still from a distance to see the daughter he had missed all these years.

Of course, Kristen had questions. She was still in shock. But something built up in Kristen as she longed for a dad, and that was to know *true love*. Pushing bitterness and hatred aside, Kristen forgave John and jumped into his arms. Kristen's mother lost it. She cried tears of joy when Kristen finally found her father again. The women in the room were sobbing just as much. What a beautiful moment for everyone.

Cathy was also in the room and couldn't believe what she was hearing. She hugged Kristen and said, "I'm so happy for you Kristen. Looks like miracles do happen. Well, what you are looking for all your life is solved for good."

"You bet, Cathy," Kristen replied.

"Now," John stated, "I got a girl to walk down the aisle."

Cathy pulled her cell phone and called Stephanie to let her know that John found his daughter and wife.

"Wow, when did you come to know this, Cathy?" Stephanie asked.

"You know the girl is no other than my roommate, Kristen," Cathy stated.

"Oh my gosh, she was the one who tried to help John to find his daughter," Stephanie exclaimed.

"Guess what," Cathy explained. "Kristen's mother forgave John, and they plan to live together."

Stephanie was so excited and wanted to tell all her friends who came to the birthday party. The news spread at a lightning speed.

* * * * *

Kristen burst into laughter through her tears and jumped with joy. The whole room clapped and cheered the bride and groom out into the wedding floor.

The priest, Foster, and his best men were aligned at the front. The wedding was sold out. There was even standing viewers and cameraman flashing their lenses. The flower girl walked, and the ring bearer nearly chucked the ring before the crowd stopped him. Kristen laughed in the moment as she was locked arms with her father, the reconciled father.

And then the song came on. "I Can Love You Like That" brought memories to both John and Kristen. As the crowd stood to their feet after the song, the anthem music played as the duo walked cordially down the aisle. Everything Kristen dreamed up as a young girl came to this very moment. John had never smiled so big, so overtaken by the moment. The crowd mirrored their faces with joy and love.

Kristen eloquently drifted up toward Foster as John gave her away, finally.

Foster and Kristen exchanged vows. The two gazed into each other's eyes with love. They said their "I dos," and Foster kissed his bride. The crowd clapped and cheered and whistled. As they finished their first kiss as a newly married couple, Foster turned around to fist-pump the crowd, which just egged everyone to shout louder.

This event was called the wedding of the decade.

Kristen and Foster jumped into their limousine to head to Barbados for their honeymoon.

* * * * *

Everything in Kristen's life was now complete. Growing up in the small town of Potomac, Illinois, she dreamed of getting married one day. And that day had finally come—but not without a cost first. She had to understand what love really wasn't to find out what love *is*. She would find love only through pain and heartache. The loss of an engagement, the turmoil of disability, finding a man who would compassionately love her for who she is, and one day walk down the aisle with a father she never knew growing up—all of this can be summed up in two words. These two words that could resonate also in your own life. Those words would be defined here as *True Love*.

Remember this—love is kind, love is patient, and it keeps no record of wrongs. It rejoices in the truth. Bears all things, believes all things, hopes for all things, and endures all things. Love always wins.

Dr. Sudhakar Ancha is a gastroenterologist who currently practices in Missouri. He was born and raised in India. Upon arrival, he completed his residency in internal medicine and then went on to complete a fellowship in gastroenterology. Throughout his education and career, he has gained a wealth of knowledge in the field of gastroenterology. Aside from his successful medical career, Dr. Ancha also has a passion for writing and the skill to tell stories. *True Love* is his first novel, which is being published by Newman Springs.